Connor McClane
from the photogr

From his form-hugging T-shirt to his worn jeans and boots to the sunglasses covering his eyes.

Kelsey tried to swallow. Once, twice. Finally, she gave up and croaked out, "Mr. McClane?"

"Yes?" He stopped to look at her, and Kelsey's only thought was that she still didn't know the color of his eyes. Brown, maybe? To match the mahogany of his hair and tanned skin. Or blue?

A dark eyebrow rose above his mirrored sunglasses. A rush of heat flooded her cheeks. "Uh, Mr. McClane—"

"We've already established who I am. Question is who are you?"

"My name's Kelsey Wilson."

He flashed a smile that revved her pulse.

Had she known her aunt was going to assign her this mission, she would have worn something different—like full body armor.

Dear Reader,

I'm sure at some point in life, we've all had a moment or two of feeling second best. Maybe it's a sibling or a friend or even a rival who has come out on top while we're stuck at the bottom.

My heroine, Kelsey Wilson, has felt this way her whole life, having grown up in her perfect cousin Emily's shadow. It takes Connor McClane, Emily's wonderfully imperfect ex-boyfriend, to bring Kelsey into the spotlight.

I hope you enjoy Kelsey and Connor's story, and here's to all the people in our lives who help us shine.

Happy reading,

Stacy Connelly

ONCE UPON A WEDDING

STACY CONNELLY

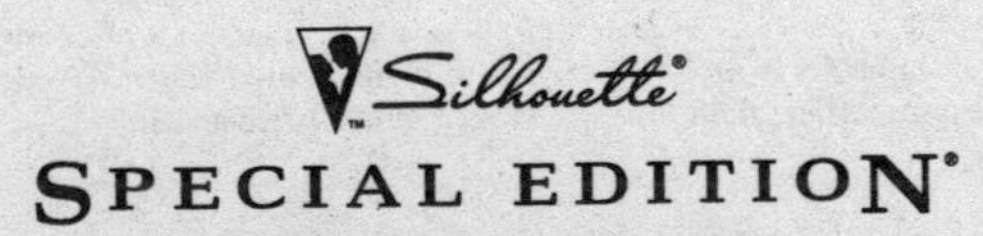

Published by Silhouette Books
America's Publisher of Contemporary Romance

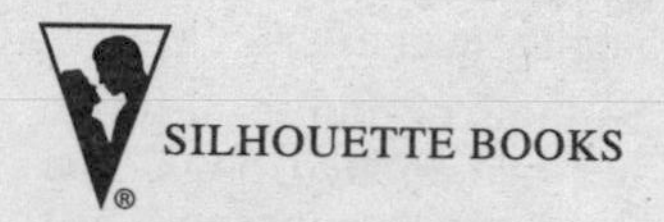

ISBN-13: 978-0-373-65474-1

ONCE UPON A WEDDING

This edition published by arrangement with Harlequin Books S.A.

Visit Silhouette Books at www.eHarlequin.com

Printed in U.S.A.

Books by Stacy Connelly

Silhouette Special Edition

All She Wants for Christmas #1944
Once Upon a Wedding #1992

STACY CONNELLY

has dreamed of publishing books since she was a kid, writing stories about a girl and her horse. Eventually, boys made it onto the page as she discovered a love of romance and the promise of happily ever after.

When she is not lost in the land of make-believe, Stacy lives in Arizona with her two spoiled dogs. She loves to hear from readers and can be contacted at stacyconnelly@cox.net or www.stacyconnelly.com.

To all my friends—

Thanks for being as excited about my dream coming true as I have been.

Chapter One

I can't believe I'm doing this, Kelsey Wilson thought as she hurried through the airport as fast as possible in her straight skirt and low-heeled pumps. Her oversized purse thudded against her side with every step. The shoulder strap caught a lock of red hair that had escaped her sensible bun, and she felt as though someone had reached out and grabbed her. Holding her back from the job she had to do.

The family is counting on you, Kelsey. Her aunt's voice rang in her mind. *You know what can happen when a woman falls for the wrong kind of man.*

Kelsey hadn't needed Aunt Charlene's reminder. She had her mother as an example. Olivia Wilson had thrown away everything for a man who left her with nothing. Olivia had been eighteen when she met Donnie Mardell—Kelsey's father, though she never thought of him in those terms. Donnie had promised Olivia a love of a lifetime, as well as freedom from her too-strict parents, and she fell for every word. When her father made her choose between Donnie and her family, Olivia chose Donnie. But while Olivia may have had stars in her eyes, Donnie had dollar signs in his. When the Wilsons offered him money to leave town, he took it without a glance back at his girlfriend or unborn child.

But Kelsey's cousin Emily hadn't fallen for the wrong man. She was engaged to Todd Dunworthy. The only son of a wealthy Chicago family, he'd come to Scottsdale to start his own company and add to his already considerable fortune. Todd was handsome, charming, and Charlene couldn't have handpicked a better son-in-law.

Kelsey had worked nonstop for the past two months to put together the perfect wedding. The dress, the flowers, the music, the cake, everything wove together like the hand-stitched Irish lace in Emily's veil. But Kelsey knew how delicate that lace was. One wrong pull, and it could all fall apart.

She refused to let that happen.

She *needed* this wedding to be amazing. She'd staked her reputation on the success of the ceremony, certain her cousin's wedding was the spotlight that would make her business shine. She'd been so sure of that she'd put most of her savings into a down payment for a small shop in Glendale. Kelsey had felt confident making the huge step. After all, her aunt and uncle were wealthy, influential people with wealthy, influential friends. Once the guests saw the job she'd done, Weddings Amour would flourish.

Even more important, her aunt and uncle would see that she, too, could succeed, that she was more than the poor relation they'd taken into their home. She'd been sixteen when her mother died, sixteen when Olivia finally admitted she was not an only child as she'd led Kelsey to believe. Olivia had an older brother, a sister-in-law and two nieces…total strangers who became Kelsey's only family.

Hold your head high, Olivia had whispered to Kelsey only days before passing away. Her face pale and gaunt, her blond hair long gone, her mother's eyes still blazed with the pride that empowered her to walk away from her family when she'd been pregnant at eighteen. *You may not have been raised as one of the wealthy Wilsons, but you're going to show them what an amazing young woman you are.*

Tears scalding her throat like acid, Kelsey had promised. She'd had no idea how difficult—how *impossible*—keeping that promise would be.

Finally, though, after eight years, she would have her chance to make good on her word. As a wedding planner, Kelsey had found her niche. She was organized, efficient, detail-oriented. Lessons learned as she scheduled her mother's doctor appointments, oversaw her medications and dealt with the insurance company served her well as she juggled caterers, musicians, photographers and the occasional Bridezilla.

Every wedding that ended in *I do* was a tribute to her mother's memory, and Emily's walk down the aisle would mean more than all the previous weddings. But before Emily could say her vows, Kelsey had to deal with one serious snag.

A sudden attack of nerves cartwheeling through her stomach, Kelsey swung her purse off her shoulder. She unzipped the center pocket and pulled out her day planner where, along with every detail of the wedding, she'd written the flight information. According to the listed arrivals, the plane from Los Angeles was on time.

Connor McClane was back in town.

Kelsey flipped to the front of the day planner and pulled out a photograph. Her aunt had said the picture was ten years old, which could account for the worn edges and creased corner. Kelsey feared there might be another reason. How many times had Emily stared at this photograph and wondered what might have been?

Kelsey had never met her cousin's ex-boyfriend, the bad boy from the wrong side of the tracks, but the snapshot said it all. Connor McClane leaned against a motorcycle, dressed head-to-toe in black—from his boots, to the jeans that clung to his long legs, to the T-shirt that hugged his muscular chest. His arms were crossed, and he glared into the camera. A shock of shaggy dark hair, a shadow of stubble on his stubborn jaw and mirrored sunglasses completed the look.

Kelsey could tell everything she needed to know from that picture except the color of Connor McClane's eyes. The man was trouble, as bad a boy as Donnie Mardell had ever been. Kelsey knew it, just like she knew Connor was better looking in a two-dimensional photo than any living, breathing man she'd ever meet.

Stuffing the picture and her day planner back in her purse, she hurried to the waiting area, where she focused on every man headed her way. He'd be twenty-nine by now, she reminded herself, four years her senior. Kelsey didn't suppose she was lucky enough that he'd aged badly or gone prematurely bald.

A beer belly, she thought, mentally crossing her fingers. A beer belly would be good.

But at the first glimpse of the dark-haired man sauntering down the corridor, her heart flipped within her chest and her hopes crashed. No signs of age, baldness or overhanging waistline…just pure masculine perfection. Her mouth went as dry as the surrounding desert.

Connor McClane had stepped to life from the photograph. From his form-hugging T-shirt, to his worn jeans and boots, to the sunglasses covering his eyes, every detail remained the same. A plane took off from a nearby runway, and the low rumble reverberating in her chest could have easily come from a motorcycle.

Kelsey tried to swallow. Once, twice. Finally she gave up and croaked out, "Mr. McClane?"

"Yes?" He stopped to look at her, and Kelsey's only thought was that she still didn't know the color of his eyes. Brown, maybe? To match the mahogany of his hair and tanned skin. Or blue? A bright, vivid contrast to his coloring.

A dark eyebrow rose above his mirrored sunglasses, a reminder that she had yet to answer him. A rush of heat flooded her cheeks. "Uh, Mr. McClane—"

"We've already established who I am. Question is, who are you?"

"My name's Kelsey Wilson."

He flashed a smile that revved her pulse. His head dipped, and she sensed him taking in the red hair she struggled to control, the freckled skin she tried to cover, and the extra pounds she sought to hide beneath the khaki skirt and boxy shirt. She saw her reflection in his mirrored glasses, a much shorter, much wider version of herself, like a carnival funhouse distortion.

Kelsey didn't feel much like laughing.

Had she known her aunt was going to assign her this mission, she would have worn something different—like full body armor. The image of what Emily might have worn to meet her former boyfriend flashed in Kelsey's mind. She shoved the pointless comparison away. Too much like trying to force Strawberry Shortcake into Barbie's wardrobe.

"Well, what do you know?" Connor stood in the middle of the corridor, mindless of the sea of people parting around him. "The Wilsons sent out a welcoming party. Heck, if I'd known I'd get this kind of reception, I might have come back sooner."

"I doubt that," Kelsey muttered.

Connor McClane had planned his return perfectly, coming back to ruin Emily's wedding. Aunt Charlene was certain of it. Kelsey knew only one thing. Her cousin had nearly thrown her future away once for this man, and she could see how Emily might be tempted to do it again.

"Don't underestimate your appeal," he told her, and though she couldn't see beyond the reflective sunglasses, she had the distinct impression he'd winked at her.

Kelsey straightened her spine to the shattering point. "My appeal isn't in question. I'm here to—"

Keep him away from Emily, Kelsey. I don't care how you do it, but keep that man away from my daughter!

"To do what, Kelsey Wilson?"

His deep voice made her name sound like a seduction, and suddenly she could think of all kinds of things to do that had nothing to do with her aunt's wishes. Or did they? How far would Aunt Charlene expect her to go to keep Connor away from Emily?

"To give you a ride from the airport," she answered with a saccharine smile. "Baggage claim is this way."

Connor patted the duffel bag slung over one shoulder. "Got everything with me."

Eyeing the lumpy bag, Kelsey wondered how dress clothes could survive such careless packing. Maybe he planned to ride his motorcycle up to the church in leather and denim, the same way he'd ridden out of town ten years ago? Unless—

"You didn't bring much with you. You must not plan to stay long."

Something in her voice must have given away her hope, because Connor chuckled. He adjusted the duffel bag and headed down the corridor, his strides so long Kelsey nearly had to jog to keep up.

"Oh, I'll be here as long as it takes," he told her with a sideways glance, "but I won't need more than a few days."

A few days. Did she really want to know? Did she really want to throw down the verbal gauntlet? Kelsey took a deep breath, partly to gather some courage, partly to gather some much needed oxygen. "A few days to what?"

"To stop Emily from marrying the wrong man."

Connor hadn't known what to expect when he stepped off the plane. He'd given Emily his flight information with the hope she might meet him at the airport. He'd wanted a chance to talk to her away from her family and her fiancé. He was realistic enough to know the whole Wilson brigade might be lined up at the gate like some kind of high-fashion firing squad. But he hadn't expected a petite redhead. He'd never imagined the Wilson genes could produce a petite redhead.

"So who are you anyway?" he asked, only to realize the woman was no longer at his side.

He glanced back over his shoulder. Kelsey Wilson stood in the middle of the corridor, her brown eyes wide, her lips adorably parted in shock. She didn't look anything like the other Wilsons, and curiosity stirred inside him. He couldn't picture her at the elegant country-club settings the status-conscious family enjoyed any more than he'd imagined himself there.

A Wilson misfit, he thought, *on the outside looking in.* Their gazes locked, and the momentary connection rocked him. Shaking off the feeling, he circled back around and asked, "You coming?"

The flush of color on her cheeks nearly blotted out her freckles. "You don't actually think you can come back here after ten years and expect to take up where you left off? You weren't right for Emily back then, and you aren't right for her now!"

As far as insults went, the words were pretty tame, especially coming from a Wilson. And it wasn't as if he had any intention of taking up where he and Emily had left off. He'd made his share of mistakes, and some—like thinking he and Emily had a chance—didn't bear repeating. Emily had been looking for someone to rescue her from the life her parents had planned for her, and he'd been young enough to think of himself as a hero.

Connor knew better now. He was nobody's hero.

Still, Kelsey's reminder stirred long-buried resentment. *Worthless. Good for nothing. Troublemaker.* Gordon Wilson had shouted them all when he'd discovered his younger daughter sneaking out to meet Connor. After being knocked around by his old man during his childhood, he knew a thing or two about male aggression and had arrogantly faced down the older man.

But Charlene Wilson's clipped, controlled words had managed to pierce his cocky facade. "From the moment Emily was born, she has had nothing but the best," Charlene told him with ice practically hanging from her words. "We have given her the world. What could *you* possibly give her?"

He'd tried to give her her freedom, the chance to live her life without bowing to her family's expectations. If someone had given his mother that same chance, things would have been different, and maybe, just maybe, she would still be alive. But when Emily made her choice, she didn't choose him. She took the easy way out—and in the end, so did he, Connor thought, guilt from the past and present mixing. But he wasn't going to fail this time. He was here to help Emily, no matter what the redhead standing in front of him like a curvaceous barricade thought.

"Look, whoever you are," he said, since she'd never explained her relationship to the Wilsons, "you didn't know me then, and you don't know me now. You don't have a clue what I'm good for."

He ducked his head and lowered his voice, not wanting to attract attention, but the words came out like a seductive challenge. He stood close enough to catch a hint of cinnamon coming from her skin. The color faded from her complexion, and her freckles stood out clearly enough to play a game of connect-the-dots. He shoved his hands into his pockets rather than give into the urge to trace a five-point star over one cheek. He tried to imagine Kelsey's reaction if he touched her. Would she recoil in shock? Or would he see an answering awareness in her chocolate eyes?

Right now, sparks of annoyance lit her gaze. "I know all I need to know. You're no good for Emily. You never were—What are you doing?" she demanded when Connor leaned around to look over her shoulder.

"Amazing. You can't even see the strings."

"What strings?"

"The ones Charlene Wilson uses to control you."

"Aunt Charlene does not control me."

Aunt Charlene, was it? He didn't remember Emily talking about a cousin, but they hadn't spent time discussing genealogy. "Funny, 'cause you sure sound like her."

"That's because we both want to protect Emily."

Protecting Emily was exactly why he was there. Adjusting the duffel bag on his shoulder, he started toward the parking garage. "So do I."

"Right." Kelsey struggled to keep up with him, and Connor shortened his stride. "Who do you think you have to protect her from?"

"From Charlene. From you." Before Kelsey could voice the protest he read in her stubborn expression, he added, "Mostly from Todd."

"From *Todd?* That's ridiculous. Todd loves Emily."

Yeah, well, Connor had seen what a man could do to a woman in the name of love. Seen it and had been helpless to stop it from happening... Shoving the dark memories of his mother and Cara Mitchell aside, Connor said, "Todd's not the golden boy the Wilsons think he is. The guy's bad news."

"How would you know?" Kelsey challenged as they stepped out the automatic doors and into the midday sunshine. Exhaust and honking horns rode the waves of heat. "My car's this way."

Connor followed Kelsey across the street to the short-term parking, where the fumes and noise faded slightly in the dimly lit garage. "I could tell from the second we met."

She stopped so suddenly he almost crashed into her back. When she turned, he was close enough that her shoulder brushed his chest, and the inane thought that she would fit perfectly in his arms crossed his mind.

Her eyes narrowed in suspicion. "You've never met Todd."

"How do you know?"

"Be-because," she sputtered. "Emily would have told me."

Despite her words, Connor saw the doubt written in her furrowed brow as she walked over to a gray sedan. The car nearly blended into the concrete floor and pylons. Between her plain vehicle and sedate clothes, he had the feeling Kelsey Wilson was a woman who liked to fade into the background.

But he was trained to notice details. He'd bet the brilliant hair she kept coiled at the back of her neck was longer and wilder than it looked, and try as they might, the shapeless clothes did little to hide some amazing curves.

"If Emily tells you everything, then you know she and Dunworthy spent a weekend in San Diego a few weeks ago, right?" At Kelsey's nod, Connor added, "Well, I drove there to meet them, and we had dinner." Keeping his voice deceptively innocent, he asked, "Emily didn't mention that?"

"Um, no," Kelsey grudgingly confessed.

"I wonder why. Don't you?" he pressed.

Not that there was much to tell, although he wasn't about to admit that to Kelsey. When he left town, he never thought he'd see Emily again. But after hearing through the long-distance grapevine that she was getting married, calling to congratulate her seemed like a good way to put the past behind him. The last thing he expected was Emily's invitation to have dinner with her and her fiancé while they were vacationing in California. But he'd agreed, thinking the meeting might ease his guilt. After all, if Emily had found Mr. Right, maybe that would finally justify his reasons for leaving Scottsdale.

But when Connor went to dinner with Emily, he didn't see a woman who'd grown and matured and found her place in life. Instead, he saw in Emily's eyes the same trapped look as when they'd first met—a look he could not, would not ignore.

Kelsey kept both hands on the wheel and her gaze focused on the road, but she was far too aware of Connor McClane to pay much attention to the buildings, billboards and exit signs speeding by. The air-conditioning blew his aftershave toward her heated face, a scent reminiscent of surf, sand and sea. His big body barely fit in the passenger seat. Twice now, his arm brushed against hers, sending her pulse racing, and she nearly swerved out of her lane.

She'd been right in thinking the man was dangerous, and not just to Emily's future or her own peace of mind, but to passing motorists, as well.

"I can't believe how much the city has grown. All these new freeways and houses..." He leaned forward to study a sign. "Hey, take this next exit."

Kelsey followed his directions, wishing she could drop him off at a hotel and call her familial duty done. Unfortunately, playing chauffeur wasn't her real purpose. Connor had flat-out told her he planned to ruin Emily's wedding. If she didn't stop him, her own business would be destroyed in the fallout. Who would trust a wedding planner who couldn't pull off her own cousin's wedding?

Panic tightened her hands on the wheel. "Where are we going?" she asked.

"My friend Javy's family owns a restaurant around here. Best Mexican food you've ever tasted."

"I don't like Mexican food."

He shook his head. "Poor Kelsey. Can't take the heat, huh?"

They stopped at a red light, and she risked a glance at him. He still wore those darn sunglasses, but she didn't need to look into his eyes to read his thoughts. He was here to win back Emily and show the Wilsons and the rest of the world they'd underestimated him all those years ago. But until then, he'd kill some time by flirting with her.

Kelsey didn't know why the thought hurt so much. After all, it wasn't the first time a man had used her to try and get to her beautiful, desirable cousin.

The light turned green, and she hit the gas harder than necessary. "Let's just say I've been burned before."

A heartbeat's silence passed. When Connor spoke again, his voice was friendly, casual and missing the seductive undertone. "You'll like this place." He chuckled. "I can't tell you how many meals I've had there. If it hadn't been for Señora Delgado..."

Kelsey wondered at the warmth and gratitude in his words. Something told her Connor wasn't simply reminiscing about tacos and burritos. An undeniable curiosity built as she pulled into the parking lot. The restaurant looked like an old-time hacienda with its flat roof and arched entryway. The stucco had been painted a welcoming terra-cotta. Strings of outdoor lights scalloped the front porch, and large clay pots housed a variety of heat-tolerant plants: pink and white vinca, yellow gazanias, and clusters of cacti.

Still checking out the exterior, Kelsey remained behind the wheel until Connor circled the car and opened the door for her. Startled by the chivalry, she grabbed her purse and took his hand. As she slid out of the seat, she hoped Connor didn't guess how rare or surprising she found the gesture.

She thought he'd let go, but he kept hold of her hand as he led her along red, green and yellow mosaic stepping stones that cut through the gravel landscape. His palm felt hard and masculine against her own, but without the calluses she'd somehow expected.

When he opened the carved door, he let go of her hand to lay claim to the small of her back. A shiver rocked her entire body. His solicitous touch shouldn't have the power to turn on every nerve ending. And it certainly shouldn't have the inexplicable ability to send her mind reeling with images of his hand stroking down her naked spine…

Full body armor, Kelsey thought once again, uncertain even that extreme could shield her from her own reactions.

Desperate to change her focus, she looked around the restaurant. A dozen round tables stood in the center of the Saltillo-tiled room, and booths lined each wall. The scent of grilled peppers and mouthwatering spices filled the air.

"Man, would you look at this place?" Connor waved a hand at the brightly colored walls, the piñatas dangling from the ceiling and the woven-blanket wall hangings.

He removed his sunglasses to take in the dimly lit restaurant, but Kelsey couldn't see beyond his eyes. Not brown, not blue, but gorgeous, glorious green. A reminder of spring, the short burst of cool days, the promise of dew-kissed grass. Without the glasses to shield his eyes, Connor McClane looked younger, more approachable, a little less badass.

"Has it changed?"

"No, everything's exactly the same. Just like it should be," he added with a determination that made Kelsey wonder. Had someone once threatened to change the restaurant that was so important to his friends?

A young woman wearing a red peasant-style blouse and white three-tiered skirt approached, menus in hand. "*Buenas tardes.* Two for lunch?"

"Sí. Dónde está Señora Delgado?"

Startled, Kelsey listened to Connor converse in fluent Spanish. She couldn't understand a word, so why did his deep voice pour like hot fudge through her veins?

Get a grip! Connor McClane is in town for one reason and one reason only. And that reason was not her.

The hostess led them to a corner booth. Kelsey barely had a chance to slide across the red Naugahyde and glance at the menu when a masculine voice called out, "Look what the cat dragged in!"

A good-looking Hispanic man dressed in a white button-down shirt and khakis walked over. Connor stood and slapped him on the back in a moment of male bonding. "Javy! Good to see you, man!"

"How's life in L.A.?"

"Not bad. How's your mother? The hostess says she's not here today?"

"She's semiretired, which means she's only here to kick my butt half the time," Javy laughed.

"I didn't think you'd ever get Maria to slow down."

"This place means the world to her. I still don't know how to thank you."

"Forget it, man," Connor quickly interrupted. "It was nothing compared to what your family's done for me over the years."

Modesty? Kelsey wondered, though Connor didn't seem

the type. And yet she didn't read even an ounce of pride in his expression. If anything, he looked...guilty.

"I'm not about to forget it, and I *will* find a way to pay you back," Javy insisted. "Hey, do you want to crash at my place while you're here?"

"No, thanks. I've got a hotel room."

Finally Connor turned back to Kelsey. "Javy, there's someone I'd like you to meet. Javier Delgado, Kelsey Wilson."

Javy did a double take at Kelsey's last name, then slanted Connor a warning look. "Man, some people never learn."

Still, his dark eyes glittered and a dimple flashed in one cheek as he said, "Pleasure to meet you, *señorita.* Take care of this one, will you? He's not as tough as he thinks he is."

"Get outta here." Connor shoved his friend's shoulder before sliding into the booth across from Kelsey. "And bring us some food. I've been dying for your mother's enchiladas." He handed back the menu without opening it. "What about you, Kelsey?"

"I'm, um, not sure." The menu was written in Spanish on the right and English on the left, but even with the translation, she didn't know what to order.

"She'll have a chicken quesadilla with the guacamole and sour cream on the side. And we'll both have margaritas."

"I'll take mine without alcohol," Kelsey insisted. Bad enough he'd ordered her lunch. She didn't need him ordering a drink for her, especially not one laden with tequila and guaranteed to go right to her head.

"Two margaritas, one virgin," Connor said with a wink that sent a rush of heat to Kelsey's cheeks. With her fair complexion, she figured she could give the red pepper garland strung across the ceiling a run for its money.

"I'll get those orders right up."

As his friend walked toward the kitchen, Connor leaned

back in the booth and gazed around the restaurant. Nostalgia lifted the corners of his mouth in a genuine smile. "Man, I've missed this place."

"So why haven't you come back before now?" Kelsey asked, curious despite sensible warnings to keep her distance.

He shrugged. "Never had reason to, I guess."

"Until now," she added flatly, "when you've come to crash Emily's wedding."

Losing his relaxed pose, he braced his muscled forearms on the table and erased the separation between them. His smile disappeared, nostalgia burned away by determination. "First of all, there isn't going to be a wedding. And second, even if there was a wedding, I wouldn't be crashing. I'd be an invited guest."

"Invited!" Surprise and something she didn't want to label had her pulling back, hoping to create some sanity-saving distance. "Who…" She groaned at the obvious answer, and the confident spark in Connor's emerald eyes. "What on earth was Emily thinking?"

"Actually, she summed up her thoughts pretty well."

Connor reached into his back pocket and pulled out an invitation. He offered it up like a challenge, holding a corner between his first and second fingers. She snatched it away, almost afraid to read what her cousin had written. Emily's girlish script flowered across the cream-colored vellum.

Please say you'll come. I can't imagine my wedding day without you.

Good Lord, it was worse than she'd thought! The words practically sounded like a proposal. Was Emily hoping Connor would stop her wedding? That he'd speak now rather than hold his peace?

"Okay," she said with the hope of defusing the situation, "so Emily invited you."

"That's not an invitation. It's a cry for help."

"It's—it's closure," she said, knowing she was grasping at straws. "Emily has moved on with her life, and she's hoping you'll do the same."

He frowned. "What makes you think I haven't?"

"Are you married? Engaged? In a serious relationship?" Kelsey pressed. Each shake of his head proved Kelsey's point. He wasn't over Emily.

Kelsey couldn't blame him. Her cousin was beautiful, inside and out. And experience had taught Kelsey how far a man would go to be a part of Emily's life.

Connor slid the invitation from her hand in what felt like a caress. "There's no reason for me not to be here, Kelsey."

Here, in Arizona, to stop the wedding, she had to remind herself as she snatched her hand back and laced her fingers together beneath the table. Not *here* with her.

The waitress's arrival with their drinks spared Kelsey from having to come up with a response. Connor lifted his margarita. "To new friends."

Rising to the challenge this time, she tapped her glass against his. "And old lovers?"

If she'd hoped to somehow put him in his place, she failed miserably. With a low chuckle, he amended, "Let's make that old friends…and new lovers."

His vibrant gaze held her captive as he raised his glass. Ignoring the straw, he took a drink. A hum of pleasure escaped him. The sound seemed to vibrate straight from his body and into hers, a low-frequency awareness that shook her to the core.

He lowered the glass and licked the tequila, salt and lime from his upper lip. "You don't know what you're missing."

Oh, she knew. The taste of a man's kiss, the scent of his aftershave on her clothes, the feel of his hard body moving against her own. How long had it been since a man had stolen her breath, her sanity? How many weeks, months? She'd probably be better converting the time into years—fewer numbers to count.

Odd how Kelsey hadn't missed any of those things until the moment Connor McClane walked down the airport corridor. No, she had to admit, she'd suffered the first twinge of—loneliness? Lust? She didn't know exactly *what* it was, but she'd first felt it the moment she'd looked at Connor's picture.

"Aren't you having any?"

Her gaze dropped to his mouth, and for one second, she imagined leaning over the table and tasting the tequila straight from Connor's lips.

"Kelsey, your drink?" he all but growled. The heat in his gaze made it clear he knew her sudden thirst had nothing to do with margaritas.

Maybe if she downed the whole thing in one swallow, the brain freeze might be enough to cool her body. She sucked in a quick strawful of the tart, icy mixture with little effect. Frozen nonalcoholic drinks had nothing on Connor McClane.

Still, she set the glass down with a decisive clunk. "You can't come back here and decide what's best for Emily. It doesn't matter if *you* don't like Todd. You're not the one marrying him. Emily is, and her opinion is the only one that matters."

Connor let out a bark of laughter. "Right! How much weight do you think her *opinion* carried when we were dating?"

"That was different."

"Yeah, because I was a nobody from the wrong side of the tracks instead of some old-money entrepreneur with the Wilson stamp of approval on my backside."

A nobody from the wrong side of the tracks. Kelsey schooled her expression not to reveal how closely those words struck home. What would Connor McClane think if he learned she had more in common with *him* than with her wealthy cousins?

Kelsey shook off the feeling. It didn't matter what they did or didn't have in common; they were on opposite sides.

"Did you ever consider that Emily's parents thought she was too young? She was barely out of high school, and all she could talk about was running away with you."

"Exactly."

Expecting a vehement denial, Kelsey shook her head. "Huh?"

One corner of his mouth tilted in a smile. "I might have been blind back then, but I've learned a thing or two. Emily was always a good girl, never caused her parents any trouble. She didn't smoke, didn't drink, didn't do drugs. No tattoos or piercings for her."

"Of course not."

From the time Kelsey had moved in with her aunt and uncle, she'd lived in her cousin's shadow. She knew all about how perfect Emily was—her fling with Connor the sole imperfection that proved she was actually human.

"Emily didn't have to do those things. She had me. I was her ultimate act of rebellion."

Kelsey listened for the arrogant ring in his words, but the cocky tone was absent. In its place, she heard a faint bitterness. "No one likes being used," she murmured, thoughts of her ex-boyfriend coming to mind.

Matt Moran had her completely fooled during the six months they dated. With his shy personality and awkward social skills, she couldn't say he swept her off her feet. But he'd seemed sweet, caring, and truly interested in her.

And she'd never once suspected he was secretly in love with her cousin or that he'd been using her to get closer to Emily. So Kelsey knew how Connor felt, and somehow knowing that was like knowing *him*. Her gaze locked with his in a moment of emotional recognition she didn't dare acknowledge.

The question was written in his eyes, but she didn't want

to answer, didn't want him seeing inside her soul. "What was Emily rebelling against?"

Connor hesitated, and for a second Kelsey feared he might not let the change of subject slide. Finally, though, he responded, "It had to do with her choice of college. She hated that exclusive prep school, but Charlene insisted on only the best. I suppose that's where you went, too."

"Not me," she protested. "I had the finest education taxpayers could provide." One of Connor's dark eyebrows rose, and Kelsey hurried on before he could ask why her childhood had differed from her cousins'. "So after Emily survived prep school…"

He picked up where she left off, but Kelsey had the feeling he'd filed away her evasion for another time. "After graduation, Gordon wanted Emily to enroll at an Ivy League school. She didn't want to, but her parents held all the cards—until I came along. I was the ace up her sleeve. Guess I still am."

The bad-boy grin and teasing light were absent from his expression, and Kelsey felt a flicker of unease tumbling helplessly through her stomach. Did Connor know something about Todd that would stop the wedding? Something that would tear apart all Kelsey's dreams for success and her chance to prove herself in her family's eyes?

"Emily invited me because her parents are pushing her into this marriage. She's pushing back the only way she knows how. She *wants* me to stop the wedding."

"That's crazy! Do you realize Emily is having her dress fitting right now? And we're going to the hotel tomorrow evening to make final arrangements for the reception? She loves Todd and wants to spend the rest of her life with him."

Leaning forward, he challenged, "If you're right, if Emily's so crazy about this guy, then why are you worried I'm here?"

A knowing light glowed in his green eyes, and history told

Kelsey she had every reason to worry. After all, on the night of her senior prom, after spending the day having her hair artfully styled and her makeup expertly applied, and wearing the perfect dress, Emily had stood up her parents' handpicked date…to ride off with Connor on the back of his motorcycle.

Having met Connor, Kelsey could see how easily he must have seduced her cousin. With his looks, charm, his flat-out masculine appeal, how was a woman supposed to resist?

And Kelsey wondered if maybe Emily wasn't the only one she should be worried about.

Chapter Two

"Honestly, Kelsey, why are you ringing the doorbell like some stranger?" Aileen Wilson-Kirkland demanded as she opened the front door. She latched on to Kelsey's arm and nearly dragged her inside her aunt and uncle's travertine-tiled foyer.

"Well, it's not like I still live here," Kelsey reminded her cousin.

Aileen rolled her eyes. "You probably rang the doorbell even when this *was* your home."

"I did not," Kelsey protested, even as heat bloomed in her cheeks. Her cousin might have been teasing, but the comment wasn't far off. She'd never felt comfortable living in her aunt and uncle's gorgeous Scottsdale house, with its country-club lifestyle and golf-course views. Before moving in with her relatives, *home* had been a series of low-rent apartments. And, oh, how she'd missed those small, cozy places she'd shared with her mother.

"I didn't want to barge in," she added.

"You're kidding, right? Like I haven't been dying to hear how things went! Did you pick up Connor? Does he look the same? Do you think—"

Ignoring the rapid-fire questions, Kelsey asked, "Where are Emily and Aunt Charlene?"

"Emily's still having her dress fitted."

"Oh, I'd love to see it." A designer friend of Kelsey's had made the dress for her cousin, but so far Kelsey had seen only drawings and fabric swatches.

For such a gorgeous woman, Aileen gave a decidedly inelegant snort as they walked down the hall. "Nice try. Do you really think you can escape without going over every detail from the first second you saw Connor right up to when you left him—" Emily's older sister frowned. "Where *did* you leave him?"

"At a restaurant."

"By himself?"

"What else could I do, Aileen? Follow him to his hotel and ask for an invitation inside?"

"Well, that would make it easier to keep an eye on him."

"Aileen!"

Waving aside Kelsey's indignation, Aileen said, "I'm just kidding. Besides, he doesn't have a car, right?"

"Like that's going to slow him down! Don't you remember the time Connor got busted for joyriding in a 'borrowed' car?" She hadn't been around then, but her aunt had remarked on Connor's misdeeds long after he'd left town. In fact, Connor's name had come up any time Emily threatened to disobey her parents. Like some kind of bogeyman Aunt Charlene evoked to keep her younger daughter in line.

Her cousin's perfectly shaped brows rose. "You don't think he's still involved in illegal activities, do you?"

"I have no idea," Kelsey said, ignoring the internal voice yelling *no.* Her automatic desire to rush to Connor's defense worried her. She was supposed to stop him, not champion him.

"You should find out," Aileen said as she led the way into the study. The bookshelf-lined room, with its leather and mahogany furniture, was her uncle's masculine domain, but even this room had been taken over by wedding preparations. Stacks of photo albums cluttered the coffee table.

"Why me?" Kelsey groaned.

"You want to help Emily, don't you?"

"Of course I do!" she insisted, even if she had to admit her motives weren't completely altruistic.

"And you want the wedding to be perfect, right?" Her cousin already knew the answer and didn't wait for Kelsey's response. "I know Mother exaggerates, but not when it comes to Connor McClane. I wouldn't be surprised if he tried kidnapping Emily again," Aileen added.

Kelsey fought to keep from rolling her eyes. "She took off with Connor on prom night and didn't come back until the next day. I think your parents overreacted."

"Maybe, but I guarantee he'll try to stop the wedding somehow." Aileen pointed an older-therefore-wiser finger in Kelsey's direction. "But don't let him fool you."

He hadn't bothered to try to fool her. Was Connor so confident he could stop the wedding that he didn't care who knew about his plan?

Walking over to the coffee table, Aileen picked up a stack of photos. "Here are the pictures Mother wants to show during the reception."

"Thanks." Kelsey flipped through images of her cousin's life. Not a bad-hair day or an acne breakout in the bunch. Even in pigtails and braces Emily had been adorable. As

Kelsey tucked them into her purse, she noticed a stray photo had fallen to the Oriental area rug. "Did you want to include this one?"

Her voice trailed off as she had a better look at the picture. At first glance, the young woman could have been Emily, but the feathered hair and ruffled prom dress were wrong. "Oh, wow."

From the time Kelsey had come to live with her aunt and uncle, she'd heard how much Emily looked like Kelsey's mother, Olivia. Kelsey had seen similarities in the blond hair and blue eyes, but from this picture of a teenage Olivia dressed for a high school dance, she and Emily could have passed for sisters.

Reading her thoughts, Aileen said, "Amazing, isn't it?"

"It is. Everyone always said—" Kelsey shook her head. "I never noticed."

"Really? But they look so much alike!"

"My mother, she didn't—" Laugh? Smile? Ever look as *alive* as she looked in that photo? Uncertain what to say, Kelsey weakly finished, "I don't remember her looking like this."

"Oh, Kelse. I'm sorry." Concern darkened Aileen's eyes. "I should have realized with your mother being so sick and having to go through chemo. Of course, she didn't look the same."

Accepting her cousin's condolences with a touch of guilt, Kelsey silently admitted Olivia Wilson had lost any resemblance to the girl in the picture long before being diagnosed with cancer. What would it have been like had her mother retained some of that carefree, joyful spirit? Kelsey immediately thrust the disloyal thought aside.

Olivia had given up everything—including the wealth and family that now surrounded Kelsey—to raise her daughter. Emily's wedding was Kelsey's chance to live up to her promise. To hold her head high and finally show the Wilsons how amazing she could be.

With a final look at the picture, Kelsey slid the photo of her mother back into one of the albums. "It's okay," she told Aileen. "Let's go see if Emily's done with the fitting."

"All right. But be warned," Aileen said as she led the way down the hall toward Emily's bedroom. "The photographer's in there."

"Really?" Kelsey frowned. "I don't remember pictures of the fitting being included. Was that something Emily requested?"

She had long accepted that her ideas and her cousins' differed greatly, but a seamstress fretting over her measurements would have been a nightmare for Kelsey, not a photo op.

Aileen shrugged and opened the door just a crack. "The photographer said it was all part of the package."

A quick glance inside, and Kelsey immediately saw what "package" the photographer was interested in. Emily stood in the middle of the bedroom, with its girlish four-poster bed and French provincial furniture. Her sheer, lace-covered arms were held out straight at her sides while the seamstress pinned the beaded bodice to fit her willowy curves. Dewy makeup highlighted her wide blue eyes, flawless cheekbones and smiling lips.

"What do you think, Mother? Will Todd like it?" Emily leaned forward to examine the skirt, testing the limits of a dozen stickpins.

The photographer, a man in his midtwenties, started snapping shots as fast as his index finger could fly. It wasn't the first time Kelsey had seen slack-jawed amazement on a man's face. Too bad she saw the expression only when her cousin was around.

"Of course he will. Audra is an amazing designer, and she created that dress just for you. It's perfect," Aunt Charlene insisted, keeping a narrow-eyed glare on the photographer.

Charlene Wilson didn't share her daughters' beauty, but she

was a tall, striking woman. She could instantly command a room with her timeless sense of style and demand for perfection from herself and those around her. Today she wore a beige silk suit that wouldn't dare wrinkle and her brown hair in an elegant twist at the nape of her neck.

Glancing down at her own clothes, a map of creases that spelled fashion disaster, Kelsey knew her aunt would be horrified by the sight. Fortunately, Charlene was far too busy to notice. Kelsey slid the door shut and walked back down the hallway with Aileen.

"I know all brides are supposed to be beautiful," Aileen said with a mixture of sisterly affection and envy, "but that's ridiculous."

"Please, I've seen pictures of your wedding. You were just as gorgeous."

Aileen gave a theatrical sigh. "True. Of course, I wasn't lucky enough to have you to plan everything. I ran myself ragged, and you make it look so easy."

Kelsey laughed even as her cheeks heated with embarrassed pleasure. "That's because I'm only planning the wedding. It's far more stressful to be the bride."

"Still, you're doing an amazing job. Mother thinks so, too, even if she hasn't told you. This wedding will make your company."

That was just what she was counting on, Kelsey thought, excitement filling her once again. "I know." Taking a deep breath, she confessed, "I put down first and last month's rent on that shop in Glendale."

Aileen made a sound of delight and threw her arms around Kelsey in a hug that ended before she could lift her stiff arms in response. After eight years, Kelsey should have anticipated the enthusiastic embrace, but somehow, both her cousins' easy affection always caught her off guard.

"That is so exciting, and it's about time! You should have opened a shop a long time ago instead of working out of your home."

"I couldn't afford it until now."

"You could have if you'd taken my father up on his loan," Aileen said.

Kelsey swallowed. "I couldn't," she said, knowing Aileen wouldn't understand any more than her uncle Gordon had. Starting her business was something she had to do for herself and for her mother's memory.

Wilson women against the world... Her mother's voice rang in her head. Opening the shop wouldn't have the same meaning with her uncle's money behind the success.

Aileen shook her head. "Honestly, Kelsey, you are so stubborn." A slight frown pulled her eyebrows together. "But something tells me you're going to need every bit of that determination—"

Kelsey jumped in. "To keep Connor McClane away from Emily. I know, Aileen. But if Emily's so crazy about Todd, what difference does it make that Connor's in town?"

Ever since he'd posed that question, Kelsey couldn't get his words out of her mind. Okay, so in her opinion, Todd Dunworthy didn't hold even a teeny, tiny, flickering match to Connor McClane. But if her cousin truly loved Todd, shouldn't he outshine every other man—including an old flame like Connor?

"Kelsey, we're talking about Connor McClane. I know you've sworn off men since Matt, but please tell me that idiot didn't rob you of every female hormone in your body!"

Even after two years, the thought of her ex-boyfriend made Kelsey cringe. Not because of the heartbreak but because of the humiliation. Still, she argued, "I'm not discounting Connor's appeal." If anything, she'd been mentally recounting every attractive feature, from his quick wit to his sexy smile and killer bod. "But if I were a week away from getting married and madly in love with my fiancé, none of that would matter."

Aileen sighed and slanted Kelsey a look filled with worldly wisdom. "It's cold feet. Every engaged woman goes through it. I called things off with Tom three times before we finally made it to the altar. You'll see what I mean when you get engaged."

The idea of Kelsey getting engaged was in serious question, but if that time ever did come, she was sure she'd be so in love she'd never harbor any doubts. "Okay, so you called off your engagement. Did you run off with another man?"

"You know I didn't."

"Well, that's my point. If Emily and Todd are right for each other, Connor's presence shouldn't matter."

"It shouldn't, but it does. You weren't here when Emily and Connor were together. He's the kind of man who makes a woman want to live for the moment and never think of tomorrow. When Emily was around him, she'd get completely caught up in the here and now of Connor McClane. But her relationship with Todd is something that can last." Aileen flashed a bright smile. "Look, you've handled prewedding problems before. All you have to do is keep Connor away. You can do that, can't you, Kelsey?"

What else could she do but say yes?

Connor scrolled through his laptop's files, going over the information he'd compiled on Todd Dunworthy. He had to have missed something.

Swearing, he rolled away from the desk in his hotel suite and pushed out of the chair. He paced the length of the room, but even with the extra money he'd paid for a suite, he couldn't go far. From the closet, past the bathroom, between the desk and footboard, to the window and back. He supposed he should consider himself lucky not to have

Kelsey Wilson shadowing his every step. An unwanted smile tugged at his lips at the thought of the woman he'd met the day before.

He'd finally convinced her to leave him at the restaurant, telling her he had years to catch up with his friend, Javy. The words were true enough, but he'd seen the suspicion in her brown eyes. He chuckled at the thought of the atypical Wilson relative. She was nothing like Emily, that was for sure. Compared to Kelsey's fiery red hair, deep brown eyes, and womanly curves, Emily suddenly seemed like a blond-haired, blue-eyed paper doll.

But no matter how much curiosity Kelsey Wilson provoked, Connor couldn't let himself be distracted.

After his relationship with Emily ended, Connor had drifted around Southern California. Different state, but he'd hung out with the same crowd. Busting up a fight in a club had gotten him his first job as a bouncer. He'd worked security for several years before taking a chance and opening a P.I. business.

Up until three months ago, he would have said he was good at his job, one of the best. That he had a feel for people, an instinct that told him when someone was lying. Listening to his gut had saved his skin more than once. Not listening had nearly gotten a woman killed.

From the first moment he'd met Todd Dunworthy, Connor had that same hit-below-the-belt feeling. And this time he was damn sure gonna listen. So far, though, his background check had merely revealed Dunworthy was the youngest son of a wealthy Chicago family. Numerous newspaper photos showed him at the opera, a benefit for the symphony, a gallery opening. And while the events and locales changed, he always had a different woman—tall, blond and beautiful—on his arm.

No doubt about it, Emily was definitely Todd's type.

"You sure you don't hate the guy just 'cause the Wilsons

love him?" Javy had pressed on the ride from the restaurant to the hotel.

Connor couldn't blame his friend for asking. And, okay, so maybe he would dislike anyone who met with the Wilsons' approval, but that didn't change his opinion. Todd Dunworthy was not the man they thought he was.

He'd spoken to several of the Dunworthy family employees and none of them were talking. It wasn't that they wouldn't say anything bad about their employers; Connor expected that. But these people refused to say a word, which told him one important thing. As well paid as they might be to do their jobs, they were even better compensated to keep quiet.

Most were lifers—employees who had been with the family for decades. But there was one woman he hadn't been able to reach. A former maid named Sophia Pirelli. She'd worked for the family for two years before suddenly quitting or getting fired—no one would say—two months ago. The silence alone made Connor suspicious, and figuring an ex-employee might be willing to talk, Connor wanted to find her.

A few days ago he'd found a lead on Sophia's whereabouts. As much as he longed to follow that trail and see where it ended, he couldn't be in two places at once. He wanted to stay focused on Todd, so he'd asked his friend and fellow P.I., Jake Cameron, to see if the former maid was staying with friends in St. Louis.

Grabbing his cell phone, he dialed Jake's number. His friend didn't bother with pleasantries. "You were right. She's here."

Finally! A lead that might pan out. "Have you found anything?"

"Not yet. This one's going take some time."

Frustration built inside Connor. Although he trusted Jake and knew the man was a good P.I., Connor wasn't used to relying on someone else. "We don't have a lot of time here."

"Hey, I've got this," Jake said with typical confidence. "I'm just telling you, she's not the type to spill all her secrets on a first date."

Connor shook his head. He shouldn't have worried. His friend had been in St. Louis for all of two days, and he already had a date with the former maid. "Call me when you've got anything."

"Will do."

Snapping the cell phone shut, Connor hoped Jake worked his cases as quickly as he worked with women. But he wasn't going to sit around waiting for Jake; he wanted to find something on Dunworthy, irrefutable proof that the guy wasn't the loving husband-to-be he pretended.

Scowling, he resumed pacing, lengthening his stride to cross the room in four steps instead of eight. Connor had never been one to back down from a fight, but some battles were lost before they'd even begun. Gordon and Charlene Wilson would never take the word of the kid from the wrong side of the tracks over their handpicked golden boy.

Dammit, he needed an insider. He needed someone the Wilsons trusted to break the bad news. He needed one of their own. He needed…Kelsey.

Connor laughed out loud at the idea, but damned if he didn't think it might work. Kelsey hadn't played a part in his past relationship with Emily. She was as unbiased a witness as he could hope to find. She had nothing at stake with Emily's wedding, nothing riding on her cousin saying "I do."

No doubt about it, Kelsey was his best shot.

The following evening, Emily twirled around the hotel's atrium, her arms outspread like Sleeping Beauty. "You were right, Kelsey. This is the perfect place for the reception. Don't you think so, Mother?"

She looked so beautiful and happy Kelsey half-expected cartoon animals to surround her at any moment. Smiling at her cousin's unfettered happiness, she breathed a sigh of relief. Connor McClane was wrong, dead wrong. Emily and Todd were meant to be.

"It's lovely," Aunt Charlene commented without looking up from her mother-of-the-bride notebook. "I knew we could count on Kelsey to find the perfect place."

"Um, thank you, Aunt Charlene," Kelsey said, surprised and pleased by the compliment. Even after eight years, Kelsey and Charlene had a tentative, tightrope relationship that had yet to get past a disastrous beginning.

When Kelsey had first come to live with the Wilsons, she'd been overwhelmed by their obvious wealth, and her cousins' beauty and grace had left her feeling outclassed. Especially when Charlene took one look at her and declared, "Someone must take this girl shopping."

Looking back now, Kelsey realized her aunt had been trying to relate to her the same way she did to her own daughters, who loved nothing more than a day spent raiding Scottsdale boutiques. But back then, as an intimidated, awkward teenager, Kelsey had suffered the pain of being seen as an embarrassment by her new family.

She'd survived the multiple fittings and outfit changes—a living, breathing, *silent* mannequin—as her aunt and a shopkeeper went back and forth over which colors, styles and accessories best suited Kelsey. But when she stood with her aunt at the register, when she saw the *hundreds* of dollars a single item cost, a sick sense of disbelief hit her stomach.

How many weeks' rent would that pair of shoes have paid for when she and her mother were living in tiny one-room apartments? How many months of food? How much better might her mother's medical have been with that kind of money?

In a quiet, cold voice, Kelsey had told the saleswoman to put every item back, before marching out of the store.

Later, once Kelsey had calmed down and realized how ungrateful her actions must have seemed, she tried to apologize to her aunt. Charlene had declared the matter over and forgotten, but never again did she offer to take Kelsey shopping.

Their relationship had yet to recover from that day. By asking Kelsey to coordinate the wedding, Charlene had helped breach the gap, but Kelsey knew this opportunity didn't come with second chances. This was her one shot.

"I've always thought this was an amazing place for a reception," Kelsey said, hearing the dreamy wistfulness in her own voice. The glass ceiling and towering plants gave the illusion of being in a tropical paradise, and from the first time she'd seen the hotel, Kelsey had known it was perfect.

Perfect for Emily, she reminded herself.

Although between having so many of her friends working the wedding and Emily's willingness to let Kelsey make so many of the decisions, the entire event was feeling more like *Kelsey's* dream wedding.

Except the choice of groom...

The insidious thought wove through her mind along with images of Connor McClane... His rebellious saunter, his too confident grin, his...*everything.*

"I hope Todd likes it." Emily lowered her arms, a small frown tugging at her eyebrows. "Do you think he will?"

"It's a five-star hotel, one of the finest in the state," Charlene said imperiously.

"I know, but Todd's family is from Chicago. They have all those historic buildings and...Todd can be particular."

Kelsey's hand tightened on her day planner at her cousin's hesitant tone. Suspicions planted by Connor's too-pointed comments threatened to sprout into tangled choking weeds, but

Kelsey ground them down. Finger by finger, she eased her grip before she left permanent indentations on the leather book.

Her cousin was a people pleaser. Of course she worried what Todd would think. "He agreed to let you make all the decisions about the wedding," Kelsey reminded Emily, who had in turn, left most of the decisions up to her. "So he must trust your choices."

"I know, but…" Emily took a look around the atrium without the excitement she'd shown moments ago. Trying to see it through Todd's particular eyes?

"But what?" Kelsey prompted gently.

"It's—it's nothing." Emily shook her head with a laugh. "I just want everything to be perfect. You understand, don't you, Kelsey?"

Yes, she knew all about trying and failing again and again. But not this time—not with Emily's wedding. "Of course I do. And your wedding will be perfect," she insisted, before an already familiar masculine voice filled the atrium and sent shivers up and down her spine.

"Hey, Em! How's the blushing bride?"

"Oh, my gosh! Connor!" Emily squealed her former boyfriend's name and ran to meet him. A broad smile on his handsome face, he caught her in his arms and spun her around. "What are you doing here?" she asked.

Keeping an arm around Emily's shoulders, Connor glanced at Kelsey. "When Kelsey said you'd be here, I had to see you."

Heat rushed to Kelsey's face. Bad enough Connor had outmaneuvered her. Did he have to rub it in in front of her aunt?

Connor McClane had been in town less than twenty-four hours, and she could already feel the familiar undertow of failure dragging her under.

"You told him we'd be here?" The words barely escaped the frozen smile on her aunt's face. Charlene would never make a scene in public. Even if it meant smiling at the man out to ruin her daughter's future.

"No! I didn't." Except she *had* told Connor Emily was making final arrangements for the reception that evening, and he would know where the reception was being held. After all, he'd been invited. "I didn't mean to," she almost groaned.

Charlene straightened her razor-sharp shoulders, taking charge of a situation that had gotten out of control. Out of *Kelsey's* control. Interrupting Emily and Connor's conversation, she said, "Mr. McClane, you'll have to excuse us. Emily has a wedding to plan."

"Mother!" her daughter protested. "Connor's come all this way to see me. We have so much to talk about. Can't this wait?"

"This is *your* wedding we're talking about, Emily! The most important day of your life."

The most important day of your life. Kelsey understood the sentiment. Every bride wanted her wedding day to be perfect, and she was doing everything in her power to see that this affair was the type every girl dreamed about, but Emily was only twenty-eight years old. Shouldn't she have something to look forward to?

Why Kelsey chose that moment to meet Connor's glance, she didn't know. He flashed her a half smile as if he could not only read her thoughts but agreed one hundred percent.

"You're right, of course, Mother." Emily turned to Connor with a smile. "I'm sorry, Connor. We don't have much time before the wedding, and there's still so much to do."

"Don't worry, Em. We'll have plenty of time to talk before then. I'm in Room 415."

"You're staying here?" Kelsey blurted the words in horror. At the hotel where not only the reception was taking place, but also the rehearsal dinner.

Connor's grin was maddening—and disturbingly enticing. "Thought it would be convenient."

"Convenient. Right." That way he could *conveniently* intrude on every event she had planned for the location and drive her insane!

"Kelsey, Emily and I can take things from here. You have…other matters to attend to now."

Her aunt's pointed look spoke volumes. Charlene could handle the final wedding details. Kelsey's job was to handle Connor McClane. She desperately clutched her day planner to her chest like a leather-bound shield. There were some things in life she could not control, but everything else made it onto a list. A methodical, point-by-point inventory of what she needed to accomplish, making even the impossible seem manageable. Nothing beat the satisfaction of marking off a completed task.

And although Kelsey certainly hadn't counted on Connor when she prioritized her checklist for Emily's wedding, as long as she kept him occupied for the next week and a half, Kelsey would be able to cross him off once and for all.

Catching a touch of her aunt's righteous indignation, she straightened her own shoulders and nodded imperceptibly. Satisfied, Charlene marched Emily out of the atrium.

Emily cast a last, longing glance over her shoulder, and the uncertainty Kelsey saw in her cousin's gaze strengthened her resolve. Aileen was right. Emily was suffering from cold feet. Her worries about her future as a wife and eventually a mother had her looking back to simpler times. Back when she could lose herself in Connor's live-for-the-day attitude.

But her cousin would only regret it if she threw away her future for a man of the moment like Connor McClane. And Kelsey could not allow Emily to make the same mistake her own mother had.

Chapter Three

"You know, Kelsey, I've never been *attended to* before."

Even with her back turned, as she watched Emily and Charlene walk away, Connor sensed the determination rolling off Kelsey in waves. Shoulders straight and head held high, she looked ready for battle. And yet when he took a closer step, his gaze locked on a curl of hair that had escaped the confining bun. The urge to tuck that curl behind her ear and taste her creamy skin nearly overwhelmed him. He sucked in what was supposed to be a steadying breath, but the air—scented with cinnamon and spice and *Kelsey*—only added to the desire burning through his veins.

Struggling to hide behind the cocky facade that had served him so well in his youth, Connor murmured, "Gotta say I'm looking forward to it."

"I don't know what you mean," she said stiffly.

"You think I don't know I'm those 'other matters' your aunt was talking about?"

Kelsey opened her mouth, looking ready to spout another unbelievable denial, only to do them both the favor of telling the truth. "You're right, Connor. My aunt wants me to keep you away from Emily."

"Charlene wants me gone and Emily happily married. There's just one problem."

"That would be you," Kelsey pointed out. "A problem easily solved if you were actually gone."

"If I leave, Emily's problems will have just begun."

"That's your unbiased opinion?"

"Yeah, it is," he agreed. "And not one your aunt and uncle are gonna listen to."

"Can you blame them?" Kelsey demanded.

No, and that was the hell of it. Connor knew *he* was the only one to blame. He knew what the Wilsons thought of him and he knew why. He could still see the look in Gordon Wilson's eyes when he offered Connor money to break up with Emily. Not a hint of doubt flashed in the older man's gaze. He'd been so sure Connor—a dirt-poor loser from the wrong side of town—would take the money.

Connor had longed to shove the money and his fist into the smug SOB's face. But he hadn't. He *couldn't.* And the pride he'd had to swallow that day still lingered, a bitter taste on his tongue.

He'd let Emily down, although from what he'd gathered during their recent conversations, she didn't know anything about the payoff. She thought their breakup had been her idea…just as she thought marrying Todd Dunworthy was her idea. But Connor knew better, and this time he wasn't going to be bought off.

"The Wilsons aren't going to listen to anything I have to say," he acknowledged. "That's where you come in."

Kelsey frowned. "I *am* a Wilson."

He hadn't forgotten…exactly. "You're different."

Drawing herself up to her five-foot-nothing height, shoulders so straight Connor thought they just might snap, Kelsey said, "Right. Different." Hurt flashed in her chocolate-brown eyes as if he'd just insulted her, when nothing could be further from the truth.

"Hey, wait a minute." Pulling her into a nearby alcove, out of the way of nearby guests, Connor insisted, "That was *not* a put-down. Your aunt and uncle turned their noses up so high when they met me, if it rained, they would have drowned. I was trailer trash, and no way was I good enough for their little girl. So when I say you're nothing like them, you can say 'thank you,' because it's a compliment."

There were a dozen words he could have said, compliments he could have used, but the stubborn tilt of Kelsey's chin told him she wouldn't have listened to a single one. Someone—her family, some guy from her past—had done a number on her.

No, words wouldn't do it, but actions… How far would he have to go to show Kelsey how attractive he found her? A touch? A kiss? The undeniable proof of his body pressed tight to hers?

"In case you've forgotten," Kelsey pointed out, her voice husky enough to let him know she'd picked up on some of his thoughts and wasn't as immune as she'd like him to believe, "according to my aunt and uncle you *kidnapped* their daughter."

"It was not kidnapping," he argued, though he'd had a hell of a time convincing the police. Fortunately Emily had backed his story, insisting that she'd left willingly. Eventually the charges had been dropped; Emily had been eighteen and legally an adult, able to make her own choices. Not that her parents had seen it that way. "But that's my point. Your aunt and uncle won't listen to anything I have to say. Which is where you come in."

"Me?"

"Right. We'll be partners."

"Partners?"

"Sure. After all, we're on the same side."

"Are you crazy? We are not on the same side!" Kelsey argued.

"I want Emily to be happy," he interjected, shaking her thoughts as easily as his sexy grin weakened her composure. "What do *you* want?"

Challenge rose in the lift of his eyebrow, but Kelsey couldn't see a way out. The trap was set, and all she could do was jump in with both feet. "Of course I want her to be happy."

"That's what I thought. Kelsey, this guy won't make her happy. He's not what he seems, and I want to prove it. The Wilsons won't believe *me,* but with you to back me up, they'll have to at least listen."

Kelsey longed to refuse. She didn't trust him. Not for a second. Oh, sure, his story sounded good, but finding dirt on Todd wasn't just a matter of looking out for Emily—it played perfectly into Connor's interests, as well.

If Connor did find some deep, dark secret to convince Emily to call off the wedding, not only would he be the hero who saved her from a horrible marriage, he'd also be there to help pick up the pieces. But if Connor couldn't find anything in Todd's past, what was to keep him from making something up? Working together, he wouldn't be able to lie. Not to mention, he'd given her a way to keep an eye on him.

Connor held out his hand. "Deal?"

Sighing, she reached out. "Deal."

Connor's lean fingers closed around her hand. Heat shot up her arm, and a warm shiver shook her whole body. Like stepping from ice-cold air-conditioning into the warmth of a sunny day.

"All right, partner."

"Not so fast." She hadn't lived with her businessman uncle for as long as she had without learning a thing or two about negotiation. "You might want to hear my terms first."

"Terms?"

Kelsey nodded. As long as Connor thought he needed her, maybe she could get a few concessions.

Instead of balking, Connor grinned. "Let's hear 'em."

"First, we're equal partners. I want to be in on this every step of the way. No hearing about anything you've found on Todd after the fact."

"No problem. From this point on, we're joined at the hip. 'Course, that will make for some interesting sleeping arrangements."

"Second, this is strictly business," Kelsey interrupted, as if cutting off his words might somehow short-circuit the thoughts in her head. But they were already there: sexy, seductive images of hot kisses and naked limbs slipping through satin sheets in her mind. She could only hope Connor couldn't read them so clearly by the heat coloring her face.

"And third?"

"Thi-third," she said, clearing her throat, "you stay away from Emily. *If* we get any dirt on Todd, *I'll* break the news to her. Until then, I don't want you filling her head with your 'bad feelings.'"

Expecting an argument, Kelsey was surprised when Connor nodded. "I'll keep my distance."

"Okay, then, we're partners." She should have experienced a moment of triumph, but all Kelsey could think was that she'd just made a deal with the devil.

Certainly, when Connor smiled, he looked like sheer temptation.

"Got to hand it to you, Kelsey, you're one hell of a negotiator. Two outta three ain't bad."

It wasn't until Connor strode away that Kelsey realized he'd never agreed to her second condition.

As Kelsey stepped into the florist shop the next morning, cool, floral-scented air washed over her. She breathed deeply, enjoying the feeling of a refreshing spa treatment without the outrageous prices. She wasn't a big believer in aromatherapy, but the stress of dealing with Connor might drive her to alternative measures. Anything to stop her pulse from jumping each time she saw him—and to keep her hormones under wraps and in control for the next ten days.

Why couldn't life be easy? Why couldn't she plan an elegant, trouble-free wedding? The kind where the biggest worry was the ice sculpture melting too quickly in the summer heat. Instead, she got Connor McClane, a man guaranteed to make women melt with nothing more than a look.

"Kelsey! Thanks so much for coming!" Lisa Remming, Kelsey's friend and the owner of In Bloom, circled the checkout counter to greet her with a hug. As always, Lisa dressed in clothes inspired by her favorite flower—bird of paradise. Her long brown hair and blue eyes were complemented by a sleeveless fiery-orange blouse and swirling olive-green skirt. "I feel so bad for calling you."

"Don't be silly." Kelsey waved off her friend's apology and pulled out her checkbook from her purse. "It's no problem."

"I still can't believe I'm doing flowers for Emily Wilson's wedding! There isn't a florist around who wouldn't kill for this job."

Hiding a smile, Kelsey teased, "Wow, who knew florists were so bloodthirsty?"

Lisa made a face, then gave Kelsey another hug. "I totally have you to thank for this."

The two women had gone to high school together, and

Lisa was one of the few people in whom Kelsey confided. By the time she'd moved in with her aunt and uncle, Kelsey had gotten accustomed to blending in and going through her teen years unnoticed. Telling her fellow students she was a long-lost member of the wealthy Wilson family would have shoved her under a microscope.

The only worse fate would have been the exclusive prep school her aunt had suggested she attend.

"I really hate asking you to do this," Lisa said as she reached behind the counter for an invoice.

"A deposit is standard practice."

"I know, but— We're talking about the Wilsons. It's not like they're going to leave me holding the bill. But with the flowers for the church and the bouquets and the boutonnieres, I have to pay my suppliers and—"

"And that's why you need the money up front." Kelsey tore off a check. The amount for the deposit alone would have depleted her own meager bank account, but Aunt Charlene had given her access to the special account established for Emily's wedding.

"Thanks." Lisa breathed a sigh of relief as she noted the deposit on the invoice. "This wedding is going to mean the world to my business." She laughed as she pressed a button on the cash register and slid the check inside. "Like I need to tell *you* that, right? You'll be flooded with calls after Emily's friends see the amazing job you're doing. Have you thought anymore about getting your own place?"

Excitement pulsing through her veins, Kelsey nodded. "I've put down first and last month's rent on the space in downtown Glendale, near the antique shops."

Lisa gave a squeal. "And you didn't even say anything! When are you moving in?"

"As soon as the current renters move out. The landlord's supposed to give me a call."

"You must be so excited! I know I was when I first opened this place. Do you have all the furniture and office equipment you'll need? Have you thought about hiring a support staff and—"

"Whoa, Lisa! Don't get carried away," Kelsey said with a laugh that sounded far too shaky.

"I'm not. Don't tell me you of all people—with your day planner and your endless lists—haven't thought of these things."

In fact, she *had,* and only days ago she'd been riding high on her plans. Now, with Connor back in town, she feared she'd put the honeymoon before the wedding, and her stomach roiled at the thought of losing control. "I don't want to get too far ahead of myself."

"What are you talking about?" Lisa challenged. "Emily's wedding is only a week and half away. You aren't too far ahead. If anything, you're behind!"

"Well, thank you for giving me that combination vote of confidence and total panic attack."

"I'm sorry. But I know how much effort you've put into this, and I want to see it pay off for you."

I want Emily to be happy. What do you *want?*

With Connor's words ringing in her head, Kelsey insisted, "Emily's happiness comes first."

"Honey, Emily's happiness *always* come first," Lisa deadpanned.

"That's not fair, Lisa," Kelsey insisted quietly.

Emily and Aileen could have turned their backs when their unknown and potentially unwanted cousin showed up to live with them. Instead, they'd done everything possible to include Kelsey. It certainly wasn't their fault she'd never fit in.

"I know." Lisa's sigh expressed an unspoken apology. "But

I also know you've played second fiddle to both your cousins for as long as I've known you. I don't want you to be so focused on Emily's wedding that you lose track of your dream."

"I haven't and I won't."

Despite her determined vow, a touch of guilt squirmed through Kelsey. She'd kept silent about renting the shop for exactly the reasons Lisa mentioned. Her aunt wouldn't want her attention on anything other than the wedding. But the shop was nothing compared to Connor McClane. The man was a living, breathing distraction.

"Emily's wedding *is* my dream," Kelsey added. "A high-profile event with an extravagant budget and built-in publicity thanks to my uncle's business contacts and my aunt's country-club friends—it's guaranteed to put my business on the map."

"I agree, and I can't believe you pulled it off in only two months!"

"It *was* short notice, wasn't it?" Kelsey asked, fiddling with the zipper on her purse.

"Yes, but you did it!"

Kelsey nodded. Thanks to working almost nonstop, she'd pulled off planning the event in a fraction of the time it normally took, but Emily had insisted on a June wedding… hadn't she?

Sudden doubts buzzed through her mind like annoying insects, unrelenting and unavoidable. Had Emily pushed for the summer wedding? Or was the idea Charlene's…or Todd's? Kelsey had been so focused on getting everything done on time, she hadn't stopped to wonder about the short engagement. Until now…until Connor had stirred up the hornet's nest of doubt.

Connor hung up the phone after ordering breakfast and ran his hands over his face. He hoped the distraction of food would wipe the nightmare from his memory. It wasn't the first time disturbing images had invaded his sleep.

The beginning of the dream was always the same. Connor watched his client, Doug Mitchell, arrive at his wife's apartment through the tunnel-eye view of a telephoto lens; only when he tried to stop the man from attacking his estranged wife, did the dream shift and alter, keeping him off balance, unsure, helpless. Sometimes he froze in place, unable to move a muscle, unable to shout a warning. Other times, he ran through air thick as quicksand, each move bogged down by guilt and regret.

But no matter how the dream changed, one thing remained the same: Connor never arrived in time to stop Doug.

A sudden knock at the door jarred the memories from Connor's thoughts. Undoubtedly the Wilsons had picked the best hotel around for Emily's reception, but no one's room service was *that* fast. Besides, he had an idea who might be on the other side of the door, and it wasn't the maid with fresh towels.

Opening the door, he summoned a smile for the woman standing in the corridor. "Morning."

Emily Wilson beamed at him, looking like a Hollywood fashion plate of old in a yellow sundress layered beneath a lightweight sweater and a scarf knotted at her neck. "Connor! I'm so glad you're here. I know I should have called first, but—"

He waved off her not-quite-an-apology and held the door open. "Come on in."

As she breezed into the hotel room and set her handbag next to his laptop, Connor was glad to see the computer logo flashing across the screen. Last thing he needed was for Emily to see the dossier on her fiancé.

Emily took her time looking around the suite's miniature living area: a cluster of armchairs and end tables encircling the entertainment center. The added touches of a stone fireplace, balcony overlooking the pool and hot tub spoke of the hotel's five-star accommodations, but Connor doubted she was impressed. After all, she'd grown up surrounded by luxury and wealth.

"What are you doing here, Em?"

"I wanted to see you." She blushed as prettily now as she had at eighteen, but somehow for Connor the effect wasn't the same.

An image of Kelsey flashed in his mind, and he couldn't help making the comparison between Emily and her cousin. It was the difference between a sepia photograph—all soft, dreamy hues—and a full-color, HD image that instantly caught the eye.

As a hotheaded teen, Emily had been his unattainable fantasy. But now it was Kelsey and her down-to-earth reality who kept intruding into his thoughts.

Like yesterday evening, when he'd stood on the balcony and watched to see if the Arizona sunsets were still as amazing as he remembered. As he watched the blazing light slowly fade on the horizon, it wasn't past evenings that came to mind. Instead he thought of the way sunshine caught the fire in Kelsey's auburn curls…

"I snuck out like when we were kids."

Emily's words jarred Kelsey from his mind. He told himself the swift kick in the gut was remembered pain and not anything current or life threatening. But, dammit, he didn't need the reminder that as far as the Wilsons were concerned, he'd never be good enough. And while Kelsey might not look like her blond-haired, blue-eyed cousins, she was still a Wilson, and some things never changed.

Judging by Emily's impish grin, she'd enjoyed reliving her youthful rebellion and the walk down memory lane. Too bad the trip wasn't so pleasant for him. Feeling his smile take a sardonic twist, he asked, "Still can't risk being seen with me in public, huh, Em?"

Her eyes widened in what looked like genuine dismay. "No, Connor! It's not like that." She reached out and grasped his arm, and the frantic expression did take him back in time, filling his thoughts with memories of the girl so desperate to make everyone else happy, she'd made herself miserable.

Relenting slightly, he leaned one hip against the arm of the sofa and reminded her, "We're not kids anymore, and we're too old to be sneaking around."

"I know." Fidgeting with her engagement ring, she added, "But I wanted to see you, and I didn't want…anyone to get upset."

"You mean Todd?" Connor asked pointedly.

"You have to understand, he's very protective of me. I'm sorry the two of you didn't hit it off when we met for dinner in San Diego last month."

Connor held back a snort of derisive laughter at the irony. No, he and Todd hadn't hit it off. In fact, at the end of the night they'd nearly come to blows. Connor could admit he hadn't walked into the restaurant with a totally open mind. It was entirely possible Connor would dislike any man who met with the Wilsons' approval on principle alone. But within fifteen minutes of meeting Todd Dunworthy, Connor had stopped thinking about the past and started worrying about Emily.

In that short span of time, Dunworthy bragged about his Scottsdale loft apartment, his top-of-the-line SUV, his various summer homes in exotic ports of call, all of which would have been little more than annoying except for one thing.

He talked about Emily the same way. She was new and bright and shiny just like the fancy Lexus he drove, and Connor hadn't been able to shake the feeling that Dunworthy wouldn't have thought twice about tossing her aside for a newer model.

And the bad feeling roiling through Connor's gut like acid

ever since he'd been hired by Doug Mitchell got so much worse. Outwardly, Doug and Todd Dunworthy had as little in common as, well, as Connor and Todd did. But from the moment he met Doug, the cold look in the man's eyes and the way he spoke about his wife set Connor's teeth on edge, too reminiscent of the way his father had talked about his mother, the bitter blame he'd placed on her for dying and saddling him with an unwanted kid to raise.

But Connor had set aside his personal feelings and taken the job. *Taken the money,* his conscience accused. If only he'd listened to his gut then…

Taking a deep breath, Connor looked out the window, hoping the daylight might dispel his dark thoughts. Only, it wasn't the sunshine that broke through the shadows, but memories of the sunset, memories of Kelsey, that eased the weight on his chest.

The spark in her dark eyes, the stubborn jut of her chin, her determination to stand up to him…even if she barely stood up to the height of his shoulder. He didn't doubt for one second she'd be a formidable opponent, and he was glad to have her on his side.

Turning his focus back to Emily, he said, "I'm sorry, too, Em." And he was. He wanted her to be happy, and he was sorry Dunworthy wasn't the man she—or more important, he suspected, her parents—thought him to be.

Something in his tone must have given his suspicions away, because Emily's already perfect posture straightened to a regal, Charlene-like stature. "Todd is a wonderful man," she insisted. "I love him. I really do, and I can't wait to be his wife."

How many times had Emily repeated that statement before she started believing it was true? The words had a mantralike sound to them. Or maybe more like the punishment meted out by a second-grade teacher: *I will not chew gum in class. I will not chew gum in class.*

"I should go," she murmured.

"Emily, wait." A knock on the door broke the tension. "Look, that's room service. I ordered way too much food. Stay and have breakfast with me."

Without waiting for her response, he stepped around her and opened the door. The waiter wheeled in the cart, filling the room with the scent of bacon and eggs. He pulled the covers off the steaming plates and revealed a meal large enough for two.

"I shouldn't," she protested, eyeing the food with a look of longing. "I need to watch what I eat or I won't be able to fit into my dress."

Connor tried to smile; dieting before a big occasion was undoubtedly a prerequisite for most women, but he didn't think it was the dress Emily had in mind. He'd shared only a single meal with Dunworthy, but he could still see the smug smile on the bastard's face as he waved the waiter and the dessert tray away with a laugh. "Gotta keep my bride-to-be looking as beautiful as ever!"

"Come on," Connor cajoled. "You're not going to make me eat alone, are you?"

Sighing, she slid onto the chair and confessed, "This smells amazing."

"Dig in," he encouraged. "Nothing like carbs and cholesterol to start the day right."

The spark in her eyes reminded him of the old Emily, and she grabbed a fork with an almost defiant toss to her head. "Thank you, Connor."

"Anytime, Em," he vowed, knowing her gratitude was for much more than a simple offer to share breakfast.

He picked up his own fork, ready to dig into the eggs,

when a hint of spice seemed to sneak into his senses. Normally sides like toast or muffins were an afterthought, something to eat only if the main meal wasn't filling enough. But the powder-sprinkled muffin on the edge of his plate suddenly had his mouth watering.

He broke off an edge and popped it into his mouth. The moist confection melted on his tongue, tempting his senses with sugar, cinnamon and...*Kelsey.*

The hint of sweet and spicy had filled his head when he stood close to her, urging him to discover if the cinnamon scent was thanks to a shampoo she used on the red-gold curls she tried to tame or a lotion she smoothed over her pale skin.

If he kissed her, was that how she'd taste?

"What's Kelsey doing today?"

The question popped out before Connor ever thought to ask it, revealing a curiosity he couldn't deny yet didn't want to admit. He set the muffin aside and shoved a forkful of eggs into his mouth in case any other questions decided to circumvent his thought process.

After taking a drink of juice, Emily said, "Oh, she's likely running herself ragged with wedding preparations, making sure everything's going to go according to plan."

Her words sent suspicion slithering down his spine. At a small, low-key wedding, the bride's cousin might be the one behind the scenes, making sure everything went *according to plan.* But not at the Wilson-Dunworthy wedding, where professionals would handle those kind of details.

"What, exactly," he asked, "does Kelsey have to do with the wedding preparations?"

Emily frowned. "Didn't she tell you she's my wedding coordinator?"

"No," he said, setting his fork aside and leaning back in the chair, "no, she didn't."

"I'm lucky to have her working on the wedding. She's amazing when it comes to organization, and she's taking care of everything."

Everything, Connor thought wryly, including him.

Chapter Four

So much for unbiased. So much for impartial. So much for finding his insider in the Wilson camp, Connor thought. Kelsey was involved in this wedding right up to her gorgeous red head.

"She started her business over a year ago," Emily was saying. "My father offered to finance the company, but she wouldn't take the loan. She's always been weird about money."

Ignoring his grudging respect for Kelsey's decision and the curiosity about her *weirdness* when it came to her family's money, Connor focused on what she was getting from the Wilson family name. "So this wedding's a big deal to Kelsey, huh?"

"Oh, it's huge! She's counting on my wedding being the launching pad for Weddings Amour. The business is totally her baby, and she loves it. Says it makes her feel like a fairy godmother, starting couples out on their own happily-ever-after."

Connor let out a snort of disbelief. He hadn't read any

fairy tales since he was six and figured it had been nearly as long since he'd believed in happily-ever-after.

"What?" Emily demanded.

"It's—nothing." He stabbed at his eggs. "The whole thing is crazy. Fairy godmothers, everlasting love, all of it—"

It was impossible. He'd seen far too many marriage vows broken from behind the telescopic lens of his camera. Those couples had likely had dream weddings, too, but the dream couldn't survive reality. And sometimes—like with Cara Mitchell—happily-ever-after turned into a living nightmare.

"Well, don't tell Kelsey her business is a joke. She takes it very seriously."

"I bet she does."

Seriously enough that Charlene Wilson had put Kelsey in charge of "attending to him." He'd overheard the comment yesterday but hadn't realized he'd be in the hands of a professional.

"Why all the questions about Kelsey?"

"Just curious." When Emily's eyes narrowed thoughtfully, he added, "I don't remember you talking about her when we were going out, that's all."

She shrugged. "I didn't know her then."

"Didn't *know* her? She's your cousin, right?"

"I, uh, I meant I didn't know her well."

"Uh-huh." Emily was a horrible liar and not much better at keeping secrets. He could have pressed. A few pointed questions, and Emily would have told him everything.

Connor refused to ask. Even as curiosity stacked one row of questions upon the next, he wouldn't ask. Not about why Emily hadn't known her own relative, not about why Kelsey had gone to public school instead of the exclusive prep schools her cousins had attended, not about why she was *weird* when it came to the family fortune.

He wasn't back in Arizona to find out about Kelsey Wilson.

Returning his focus to that goal, he asked, "What's Todd up to today? He must have a lot of free time on his hands while you and your mother and Kelsey take care of all the wedding details."

"Oh, no. He has a meeting this morning. He'll be at his office most of the day."

"Really?" Now, this could be something. Connor forced himself to take a few bites of waffle before he asked, "What kind of meeting?"

"I'm not sure." A tiny frown tugged her eyebrows. "Todd doesn't tell me much about his work." Laughter chased the frown away. "Just as well. I'd be bored silly."

"I doubt that. You're smart, Emily. Smarter than you give yourself credit for."

"Thank you, Connor," she said softly.

"How'd you two meet anyway? I don't think you've said."

"At a department store." She smiled. "We were both shopping for Christmas presents for our mothers, but he didn't have a clue. Finally he asked me for help. It was really cute."

"Hmm. Almost as cute as when we met."

"Oh, you mean in that sleazy bar where you had to fight off those bikers who were hitting on me?"

"A bar you weren't old enough to be at in the first place," Connor pointed out.

"Luckily you were there to rescue me," she said, lifting her glass in a teasing toast.

"Yeah, lucky," Connor agreed as he tapped his own glass against hers.

Emily might not know it, but he was here to save her again.

The tiny butterflies taking flight in Kelsey's stomach as she drove toward the hotel turned into radioactive monsters by the time she stepped into the lobby. She'd been crazy to make a deal with Connor McClane. Somewhere along the way she was going to lose her soul.

Although they hadn't made plans to meet this morning, the best way to keep an eye on Connor was to embrace their partnership. As she walked by the three-tiered fountain toward the elevators, the doors slid open. Kelsey gasped and ducked into an alcove—the same alcove to which Connor had pulled her aside the day before—and watched in disbelief as her cousin walked by.

What was Emily doing at Connor's hotel?

Her cousin rarely left the house before noon, and it was barely nine o'clock. What was Emily doing up so early? Or had she stayed out too late? Kelsey's stomach churned at the thought. She hated to think her cousin would be so susceptible to Connor's charms. *And what about you?* her conscience mocked. *How easily did you agree to work with Connor in this very spot?*

But that was different! That was about business and keeping an eye on Connor and keeping him away from Emily…not that Kelsey had done a bang-up job at either so far.

Emily slipped on a pair of sunglasses and smiled at a bellboy, who nearly tripped over his feet as she walked by. She didn't look as if she'd rolled out of bed with her ex-lover, but then again, Kelsey had never seen Emily look less than perfect. Ever.

Kelsey stayed hidden as her cousin sashayed across the lobby and out the automatic doors, then made a beeline for the elevator. "So much for his promises," she muttered as she jabbed the Up button.

"But why am I even surprised?"

She stomped out of the elevator on the fourth floor. Had she really believed Connor would keep his word?

Maybe she had. Which only went to prove how some

people never learned. Rapping on Connor's door hard enough to bruise her knuckles, she thought she'd be better off banging her head against the wood.

"Kelsey." Opening the door, Connor greeted her with an assessing look and not an ounce of shame. Bracing one arm on the doorjamb, he said, "I'm surprised to see you here."

"Are you?" Determined to ignore the masculine pose that could have come straight from some sexy man-of-the-month calendar, she ducked beneath his arm and made her way inside. She refused to have an argument in the hall where any guest, bellhop or room-service waiter might walk by. "If I'd shown up a few minutes earlier, it would have been a regular family reunion."

"You saw Emily?"

"So much for your promise to keep your distance!"

Connor frowned. "I said I'd stay away. I can't help it if she comes to see me."

"Right. And I'm sure she forced her way inside your hotel room. Probably tied you up and had her way with you, too."

Connor pushed away from the door and stalked toward her with that challenging expression still in his eyes. "That would really mess up your plans, wouldn't it?"

"She's engaged, Connor. Doesn't that mean anything to you?"

"Yeah. It means she's about to make a mistake."

Connor stepped closer, and the only mistake Kelsey could concentrate on was her own in thinking she could confront Connor face-to-face and not be overwhelmed by his masculine sensuality. He hadn't shaved and the morning stubble only made him that much more appealing. Worse, she could practically feel the erotic scrape of whisker-rough skin against her cheeks, her neck, her breasts—

Afraid he could read her every thought by the glow in her cheeks, Kelsey ducked her head. Her gaze landed on the nearby breakfast tray, on a white coffee cup and a pink bow-shaped smudge left by Emily's lipstick. The mark may have been left on Connor's cup, not on the man himself, but the reminder that Emily had been there first doused Kelsey like a bucket of ice water. "Emily's only mistake was inviting *you.*"

"Yeah, I bet that's tough on you, isn't it? When you told me yesterday working together would be strictly business, I didn't realize that meant you were getting paid."

"So I'm coordinating Emily's wedding. Don't act all offended like it was some big secret. I thought you already knew."

"Yeah, well, I didn't. If I had—"

"You would have what?"

Scowling at her, he said, "Look, if you want to work together, I need to know you care more about your cousin than you do about your business."

If she wanted to work together! Just yesterday, she thought agreeing to work with Connor was possibly the most foolish thing she'd ever done. And now she had to fight to keep the opportunity?

Yes! a voice inside her head argued. *Because it's the only one you'll get. How else will you keep an eye on him? How else will you keep him from stopping the wedding?*

"Of course I care about Emily."

A sardonic twist of a smile lifted one corner of Connor's mouth. Darn him for making even sarcasm look sexy! "I know you care about her. The question is, do you care enough to put her first over everything else you want?"

The intensity in his eyes transformed the question from a challenge about her loyalty to Emily into something more personal. Something dark and revealing about his past. *Prove that you care…*

It was a test Emily had failed. She hadn't cared enough, or

she'd cared about her family's approval more. Was Emily the only woman who hadn't passed, Kelsey wondered, or were there other women who hadn't given Connor the proof he needed?

"You can't prove you care about someone," she stated flatly. "Not in words. Actions show how you truly feel."

Like Connor showing up for Emily's wedding…and Emily showing up at Connor's hotel room. Trying not to think what those actions meant, Kelsey continued, "I'm here. That alone should prove—"

"That you're a clever businesswoman? I already knew that."

Tightening her grip on her purse strap, Kelsey fought for control. She couldn't pretend she didn't have a lot riding on Emily's wedding.

As she racked her brain for a way to prove her loyalty, Kelsey realized nothing she said would be enough. Meeting his gaze, she stated, "I can't prove it to you, Connor. Because love and caring aren't about proof. They're about faith. So, if I'm supposed to trust your gut when you tell me Todd isn't right for Emily, you're going to have to trust me when I tell you Emily's happiness matters most."

With his gaze locked on hers, Connor stayed silent long enough for Kelsey to anticipate half a dozen responses. Would he laugh in her face? Turn away in cynical disgust?

Seconds ticked by, and she held her ground by pulling off a decent imitation of her aunt. She kept her back straight, her head held high, and still managed to look down her nose at a much taller Connor.

He ruined the hard-won effect with a single touch, tracing a finger over her cheek. The steel in her spine melted into a puddle of desire.

"Good to have you back on the team," he said softly. "We have work to do."

* * *

Connor knew he'd crossed the line when Kelsey's eyes widened to a deer-caught-in-the-headlights look. He needed to back off. If he pushed, she'd bolt. But it was the urge to ignore his own boundaries that had him pulling back even further.

If anyone could make him *want* to trust again, Kelsey might. And that sure as hell wasn't the kind of thought a man wanted to have while sober. Especially not a man like him about a woman like her.

Kelsey was a Wilson, and he'd already learned his lesson when it came to how Wilson-McClane relationships ended. He knew better than to make the same mistake twice… Didn't he? Just because he'd indulged in a minor fantasy—discovering the five freckles on Kelsey's cheek *did* combine to make a perfect star—didn't mean he was losing his grip on the situation. He had everything under control, even if that star-shaped outline made him wonder what other patterns he might find on Kelsey's body….

Far too aware of the bed only a few feet away and Kelsey's teasing scent, that alluring combination of cinnamon and spice, Connor redirected his focus. "Are you hungry? I could order more room service."

"No, thank you." Her words were too polite, bordering on stiff, and they matched her posture.

"All right," he said, thinking it just as well they get out of the hotel room before he ended up doing something as stupid as touching Kelsey…and not stopping. "But you really don't want to go on a stakeout on an empty stomach." Connor didn't know if his sudden announcement loosened anything, but Kelsey definitely looked shaken.

"Stakeout?" Echoing the word, her brown eyes widened.

"Don't worry. We'll stop for staples along the way." He grabbed her hand, pulled her from the room and out into the hall.

She protested every step of the way and all throughout the elevator ride down to the lobby. "Are you insane? I am *not* going on a stakeout."

Her voice dropped to a hiss as the elevator door opened, and she even managed a smile at the elderly couple waiting in the lobby.

"You agreed to this, remember? Equal partners?"

As he strode across the lobby, Connor realized Kelsey was practically running to keep up with his long strides, and he slowed his steps.

Jeez, it'd be faster if he picked her up and carried her. A corner of his mouth lifted at the thought of Kelsey's reaction if he tried. "You really are tiny, aren't you?"

"I— What?"

She bumped into him when Connor paused for the automatic doors to open. He had the quick impression of soft breasts against his back before Kelsey jumped away.

Tiny, he decided as he looked over his shoulder with an appreciative glance, but curved in all the right places.

Something in his expression must have given his thoughts away. Kelsey glared at him. "I am not going on a stakeout."

"How are we going to find anything out about Todd if we don't watch him?"

"I thought you'd hire someone!"

"Right. Because the Wilsons would believe whatever some guy I *paid* has to say about their golden boy."

Score one for the away team, Connor thought, when Kelsey stopped arguing. Pressing his advantage, he guided her outside. "Besides," he added, "staking people out is what I do."

"You—you're a cop?"

He couldn't blame her for the shock in her voice and gave a scoffing laugh. "No. I'm a private investigator. Turns out we're both professionals," he said. "And if it makes you feel any better, I do have a friend working another lead. But he's in St. Louis."

"What's in St. Louis?"

"A maid who used to work for the Dunworthy family. She either quit or was let go a few months ago."

"So?"

"She pretty much disappeared after that, and I want to hear what she has to say about her former employers."

Midmorning sunlight glinted off the line of luxury cars brought around by the valets: Lexus, BMW, Mercedes. He'd come a long way from his bike days. Too bad. He would have enjoyed getting Kelsey on a Harley. Once she loosened up a bit, she'd love the freedom of hugging the curves, wind whipping through her hair, speed pouring through her veins. He could almost feel her arms around his waist…

Kelsey waved toward the visitor's lot. "We can take my car."

It didn't look like loosening up would happen anytime soon. "Sorry, sweetheart, but I'll bet Dunworthy has already seen your car."

Connor signaled a valet, and within minutes a vintage black Mustang pulled up to the curb. Seeing the question in Kelsey's eyes, he explained, "It's Javy's. Something less flashy would be better for surveillance, but borrowers can't be choosers."

He tipped the valet and opened the passenger door for Kelsey. When she looked ready to argue, he said, "Todd has a big meeting at his office." He'd looked up the address after Emily left. "I'm curious to find out who it's with. How 'bout you?"

As she slid into the passenger seat, Kelsey muttered something he couldn't quite make out.

Connor figured it was just as well.

* * *

"I cannot believe I'm doing this," Kelsey muttered from her slumped-down position in the passenger seat.

"You've mentioned that," Connor replied.

They were parked in a lot across the street from Todd's office. The row of two-story suites lined a busy side street off Scottsdale Road, the black glass and concrete a sharp contrast to the gold and russet rock landscape, with its clusters of purple sage, flowering bougainvillea and cacti. Connor had circled the building when they first arrived, noting all the building's entrances and confirming Todd's car wasn't in the lot.

"What if someone sees us?"

"What are they going to see?" he retorted.

She supposed from a distance the car did blend in. Thanks to heavily tinted windows, it was unlikely anyone could see inside. Tilting the vents to try to get a bit more air to blow in her direction, Kelsey admitted, "This is a bit more boring than I expected."

"Boring is good," Connor insisted. Despite his words, he drummed his fingers against the steering wheel in an impatient rhythm, clearly ready for action.

"I'm surprised Emily didn't tell me more about your job."

"Why would she?"

"Because to anyone not sitting in this car, being a P.I. sounds exciting." When Connor stayed silent, she asked, "Do you like it?"

"Yeah. Most of the time."

The tapping on the steering wheel increased like the sudden peaks on a lie detector, and Kelsey sensed he was telling her not what he thought she wanted to hear, but what he *wanted* to believe. Something had happened to change his mind about the job she suspected he'd once loved. "It must be difficult. Seeing so much of the darker side of life."

"It can be. Sometimes human nature is dark, but at least my job is about discovering the truth."

Was it only her imagination, or had he emphasized that pronoun? Subtly saying that while he pursued truth and justice, she— "You think *my* job is about telling lies?"

"Selling lies," he clarified.

"I promise a beautiful wedding and give the bride and groom what they're looking for. That's not a lie."

"Okay," he conceded, "maybe not the beautiful wedding part, but the sentiment behind it? Happily-ever-after? Love of a lifetime? Till death do us part? Come on!"

"Not every marriage ends with the bride and groom riding off into the sunset. Real life comes with real problems, but if two people love each other, they work it out."

He snorted. "Not from my side of the video camera, they don't."

Irritation crackled inside her like radio static—annoying, incessant and almost loud enough to drown out a vague and misplaced feeling of disillusionment. All these years, she'd heard about Connor and Emily as a modern-day Romeo and Juliet, but the story of star-crossed lovers lost all meaning if one of the players didn't believe in love.

And while Kelsey's faith might have been shaken by what happened with Matt, she still longed for those happily-ever-after and love-of-a-lifetime dreams Connor cynically mocked.

"My aunt and uncle never believed you loved Emily," she said, disappointed. "Everything you've said proves them right."

"Your aunt and uncle weren't right about me—no matter what they think."

Dead certainty ricocheted in his voice, and Kelsey regretted the tack she'd taken. Too late to back down and far too curious about what made Connor tick, she pressed, "Either you believe in love or you don't. You can't have it both ways."

"I just don't want to see Emily get hurt. That's why I'm here."

She opened her mouth, ready to push further, when Connor pulled the handle on the driver's-side door. "I'll be right back."

Kelsey grabbed his arm. "Wait! Where are you going?"

"To check the rear lot. Todd might have pulled in back there while we've been watching the front." With one foot already on the asphalt and refusing to meet her gaze, Connor seemed more interested in escaping her questions.

"I'm coming with you." She scrambled to unlock the passenger door. When she sensed an oncoming protest, she said, "Partners, remember? You're the one who dragged me along. You aren't leaving me now."

"Forget it! He'll recognize you."

"Todd knows what you look like, too," she argued as she turned back toward him.

"Fine," he bit out as he dropped back into the seat, "but there's something you have to do first."

Thanks to her questions, a noticeable tension vibrated through Connor, evident in his clenched jaw and the taut muscles in the arm he'd braced against the wheel. But the tension gradually changed, not easing, but instead focusing to a fine, definitive point—one that seemed wholly centered on her.

His intense gaze traveled over her hair, her face, her mouth… The gold flecks in his green eyes glowed, and Kelsey's skin tingled as if warmed by his touch. Surely he wouldn't try to kiss her. Not here, not now! Time raced by with each rapid beat of her heart, a single question echoing in her veins.

Why *didn't* he kiss her? Right here, right now—

Her pulse pounded in her ears, drowning out the sound of passing traffic. The heat shimmering on her skin could put the mirage hovering above the asphalt to shame. Shifting his body in the driver's seat, Connor eased closer. The scent of his aftershave, a clean fragrance that called to mind ocean breezes and sun-kissed sand, drew her in. Like waves rushing to the shore, helpless to resist the undeniable pull, she reached for him….

But instead of a roll on the beach, Kelsey crashed against the shoals, her pride battered against the rocks when Connor suddenly turned away. He twisted his upper body between the seats and reached into the back. "Here, take this."

Kelsey stared dumbly at the baseball hat he held.

"See if you can cover your hair."

Her hand was still raised in an attempt to reach out and capture a passion obviously only she felt. An admission of her willingness to make a fool of herself.

Kelsey jerked the hat from Connor, eager to grab hold of anything to save face. "Do you really think this will make a difference?"

"A huge one." Almost reluctantly he added, "Your hair is unforgettable."

But he'd forget all about her and her hair once Emily was a free woman again. Unforgettable. Yeah, right.

Kelsey didn't realize she'd spoken the words until Connor murmured, "It's the kind of hair a man fantasizes about. Trust me."

But she couldn't. She'd nearly made a fool of herself seconds ago, and in case she ever forgot, she had the living, breathing epitome of Connor's perfect woman as her cousin. Kelsey couldn't compare; she never had.

Jerking back toward the door to put as much room as possible between them, she shook back her hair and pulled it away from her face with sharp, almost painful movements. Unable to hide behind her long locks, she felt exposed, vulnerable. Even more so when Connor's gaze remained locked on her features.

"How's that?" she asked, as she twisted her hair into a bun and shoved the bright red Diamondbacks cap into place. When

Connor continued to stare, Kelsey fisted her hands in her lap to keep from yanking off the ridiculous hat. Finally, she demanded, "What?"

Shaking his head, Connor seemed to snap out of his stupor. "I hadn't realized how much you look like Emily."

His words hit like a punch in the stomach. Look like Emily? Not a chance. She'd seen the disappointment in the Wilsons' faces when they first saw her. If Emily and Aileen were beautiful Barbie dolls, then Kelsey was clearly supposed to be Skipper, a younger, blonder version. But she looked *nothing* like her cousins, a point driven home at every Wilson function, with every meeting of their friends and associates. The surprise—if not flat-out disbelief—when Kelsey was introduced as one of the Wilsons.

I hope they had her DNA tested, Kelsey had heard one uninformed, high-society snob whisper. *It wouldn't surprise me if that girl ended up being a con artist out for the family fortune.*

Kelsey had struggled to hold her head high and hold back the tears when she'd wanted to lash out at the woman. She was every bit her mother's daughter, *not* her father's, and inside she was as much a Wilson as Gordon, Aileen and Emily. But outside—where it counted—she couldn't be more different.

"Give me a break!" She tried to laugh off the remark, but the fake sound stuck in her throat. "Emily and I look nothing alike! She's tall and thin and blond and—beautiful!"

Her voice broke on the last word, and Kelsey had never been so close to hitting anyone. Giving in to the impulse, she socked Connor in the shoulder. She had a quick impression of dense muscle and bone, but he caught her hand before she could fool herself into thinking she could do more damage.

"Hey!" A quick tug of her arm had her falling against him. "So are you!"

"Tall? Blond?" Kelsey shot back sarcastically.

"Beautiful!" he retorted.

"But I'm not—"

"Not Emily?" he interjected softly. He brushed an escaping strand of hair—her unforgettable hair—back from her face, and the touch she'd only imagined became reality as he traced his index finger over her eyebrow, across her cheekbone, and skimmed the corner of her mouth. Heat and hunger combined with a tenderness that snuck beneath her defenses. "There's more than one ideal for beauty, Kelsey."

Still pressed against his muscular chest, she knew Connor was the epitome of masculine beauty for her, and she had the devastating feeling that would never change, even years from now. He was the best of the best, and she was a long shot, the dark horse.

"Stop it," she whispered furiously.

"You don't have to be Emily. You can just be yourself."

The deep murmur of his voice reached inside and touched that vulnerable place, but this time instead of opening old wounds, his words offered a healing balm. And meeting his gaze, Kelsey realized he understood her vulnerability in a way no one else could because he'd felt the same way. He'd never been good enough to date the daughter of the wealthy Wilsons, and she had never felt good enough to *be* one of the wealthy Wilsons.

"Connor…" Just one word, his name spoken in a hushed whisper, broke the connection. He blinked, or maybe Kelsey did, because when she looked again, his sexy smile was back in place, all sense of vulnerability gone. "Except for right now. Right now you have to be someone Todd won't recognize."

"Right." Kelsey pulled back, and Connor let her go. She might not have a sexy smile to hide behind, but she could be businesslike and professional…or as businesslike and professional as a wedding coordinator spying on a future groom could be.

"Come on," she muttered as she tugged the brim lower. She didn't know if she'd need the hat to hide her identity from Todd, but maybe she could use it to hide her emotions from Connor. "Let's do this."

She climbed from the car and was headed straight for the building by the time Connor caught up with her. Grabbing her hand, he said, "This way."

With Connor leading the way, they walked half a block before crossing the street and doubling back behind Todd's building. But the lot was empty except for some abandoned crates and an overflowing Dumpster.

"Let's go. Todd's meeting must have been canceled," Kelsey said. She walked around to the front of the building without bothering to take the circular route that got them there, her low heels striking the steaming pavement.

Connor caught up to her as she reached the front of the building. "Look, I admit this was a dud, but—" He cut off with a curse.

Kelsey didn't have time to take a breath before he shoved her into a recessed doorway and nearly smothered her with his body. Her vehement protest came out a puny squeak.

"Don't move." The husky whisper and warm breath against her ear guaranteed she couldn't take a single step without falling flat on her face. "Todd's pulling into the parking lot."

No, no, no! This could not be happening! Swallowing against a lump of horror, Kelsey fisted her hands in his T-shirt and tugged. "Let's go," she hissed.

"Can't. He'll see us if we move. Just…relax."

Despite the advice, every muscle in his body was tense, primed and ready for action. But it was Kelsey who jumped when the car door slammed. "He'll see us."

"No, he won't. He's heading for his office."

She had to take Connor's word for it. With his body

blocking every bit of daylight, she couldn't see beyond his broad shoulders. Too bad the rest of her senses weren't so completely cut off. Instead, the scent of his sea-breeze aftershave combined with potent warm male, and the masculine heat of Connor's chest burned into her skin where he made contact with her. Kelsey locked her knees to keep from sinking right into him.

Heart pounding in her ears, she whispered, "Where is he now?"

"Unlocking the door."

She felt as much as heard his low murmur and hissed, "We should go." Right now, before the heat went straight to her head and she did something unforgivably stupid, like melt into a puddle of desire at Connor's feet.

Chapter Five

"I am not meant for a life of crime."

Seated in a restaurant not far from Dunworthy's business, Connor pressed a beer into Kelsey's hand. That she took it without complaint told him how much the incident at Todd's office had shaken her.

Their near miss had lasted only seconds. Connor had pulled Kelsey toward the car immediately after Todd entered the suite; she'd barely ducked inside the Mustang's ovenlike interior when he came back outside. Connor might have suspected the other man sensed something wrong if not for the way he sauntered out to his top-of-the-line SUV without checking his surroundings. If he had, it was a good bet he would have caught sight of Connor sliding into the driver's seat only a few yards away.

Connor had wanted to follow him, but with Kelsey along, the risk wasn't worth it. Not that it was her fault they'd nearly been spotted. No, Connor took full blame. He'd let Kelsey distract him. He could have driven her back to the hotel and her waiting car but had instead veered off to the restaurant, which had a bar. He figured she could use a drink. After standing in the doorway with the Arizona sun roasting his back, Connor could use a cold shower, but a cold beer was the next best thing.

Liar, a mocking voice jeered. The hundred-plus temperature was a killer, but it was the feeling of Kelsey's body pressed to his that heated his blood.

"Hate to tell you, but we didn't break any laws."

She took a long pull on the bottle, then set it back on the bar with an audible clunk. "We were trespassing."

Hiding his smile behind the beer bottle, he bit back a burst of laughter. "The parking lot is public property. We had every right to be there."

"Oh." Kelsey stared thoughtfully at the bottle. He couldn't tell if she was relieved or disappointed. Finally, she looked up, her expression resolute. "Okay, so maybe what we did wasn't illegal, but—but it was unethical. It isn't right to go around spying on people. Especially when they aren't doing anything wrong. And I don't have time to waste chasing Todd or any of your ghosts around town." She slid out of the booth.

Connor frowned. "Hey, this doesn't have anything to do with me."

"Bull. You're out to prove to Aunt Charlene and Uncle Gordon you're much better for Emily than their handpicked golden boy."

Connor recoiled against the padded booth. Was Kelsey right? Did coming back to Arizona have more to do with salvaging his ego than protecting Emily?

No. No way. He wasn't nearly that pathetic. Unfortunately,

Kelsey had almost reached the door by the time he came to that conclusion. "Kelsey, wait!"

"Hey!" The bartender called after him. "Those beers weren't free, you know."

Swearing, Connor dug out his wallet, threw a handful of bills on the bar, and raced after Kelsey. The sunlight threatened to sear his corneas after the dimly lit bar, and he shaded his eyes against the glare. "Kelsey!"

The rush of nearby traffic nearly drowned out his voice, but Connor doubted that was why she didn't stop. Jogging after her, he caught her as she reached the car. It took a second longer to realize he had the keys, and she couldn't go anywhere without him.

Dammit, what was it about Kelsey that made him so crazy? He hadn't felt like this since—since Emily.

You're a fool, boy. Just like your old man. His father's voice rang in his head. *The both of us always want to hold on to what we can't have.*

Thrusting the comparisons aside, he said, "Look, I know this afternoon was a bust, but this isn't about me."

"Really?" Disbelief colored her words, and Connor fought a flare of irritation mixed with admiration. Had to respect a woman who wasn't easily snowed.

Taking a deep breath, he forced the irritation aside. He couldn't risk losing Kelsey as a partner. That was the reason he didn't want her to leave. It had nothing to do with wanting to spend more time with the woman who had him so fascinated.

Yeah, right, his conscience mocked. Back at Todd's office, he'd been tempted to forget all about the other man and prove to Kelsey just how beautiful she was. But he refused to make out with a woman in a parked car. Especially *not* Javy's car, the same vintage automobile he'd borrowed to take Emily out on dates all those years ago.

He wasn't that same punk kid anymore, even if he was once again lusting after one of the wealthy Wilsons.

"Let me buy you lunch, and I'll tell you what I *do* know about Todd."

Back in the restaurant, under the bartender's watchful eye, Connor and Kelsey placed their orders. As soon as the waitress walked away, Kelsey leaned forward and prompted, "Okay, let's hear it."

"First, did Emily ever tell you how we met?"

Kelsey's gaze dropped as she fiddled with her napkin. "She might have."

"Well, just so you have the whole story, Emily went to a bar. She was underage and in over her head. Some guys started hitting on her. She tried to shrug it off, but she was afraid to tell them to go take a hike. Because that wouldn't have been *nice.* But I could see the panic in her eyes. She was waiting for someone to step in and save her."

"And so you did."

"And so I did." Leaning across the table, he covered Kelsey's hand, intent on claiming her complete attention. Only when her eyes widened perceptibly did Connor realize he'd nearly erased the two-foot distance separating them. He was close enough to count the freckles dotting her upturned nose, to catch hold of her cinnamon scent. Her startled gaze flew to meet his, and as the spark of attraction he saw in her brown eyes flared to life inside him, Connor was the one having a hard time staying focused.

"The, uh, thing is—when I look at Emily now, I see that same panic. She's in over her head, letting herself get pushed along because she's too *nice* to stand up for herself."

"So you rode back into town, ready to play the hero."

"I'm no hero," Connor stated flatly, leaning back in the booth and pulling his hands from Kelsey's. The softness of her skin threatened to slip beneath his defenses, making him weak. The passion in her eyes when she spoke about everlasting love and dreams coming true made him want to believe though he knew better.

Even if he didn't have countless professional examples of love gone wrong to draw from, he also had his parents' as proof of love's fallibility. During their short-lived marriage, his parents drifted so far apart that in the end, neither his father nor Connor had been able to pull his mother back to safety.

If only she'd listened— Helplessness roiled in his gut, but he'd learned his lesson.

It would take more than words to keep Emily safe; he had to have proof. But right now, words were all he had to convince Kelsey. The only way to do that would be to open up and be completely honest. "I didn't expect to like Todd when I met him. I walked into that restaurant in San Diego knowing he's the Wilsons' golden boy and everything I'm not."

"Now who needs the lesson about being himself?" Kelsey murmured.

"Nothing like having my own words shoved back in my face," he said with a smile, which fell away as he realized how much they did have in common, how easily Kelsey understood him. Their gazes caught and held, the spark of desire running on a supercharged emotional current.

A touch of pink—sunset pink—highlighted Kelsey's cheeks, and she dropped her gaze. "Not shoving, exactly. More like gently tossing."

The waitress arrived with their food, breaking the moment and giving Connor a chance to refocus on what he wanted to say. "This is about more than disliking Dunworthy on sight. It's about the way he treats people he thinks are beneath him."

"Like who?"

"Like the valet he was pushing around after we left the restaurant."

"What?"

"I was pulling out of the lot when I saw Todd grab the kid and shove his face an inch from the bumper to show where he'd *dented* the car." Leaning forward, Connor added, "It was a rental, Kelsey. You can't tell me he had any clue whether that scratch was there before or not. But he's the type of guy who likes to intimidate people, especially people who can't or won't fight back."

"What did you do?"

"Jumped out of my car and pulled him off."

"And Todd actually grabbed this kid in front of Emily?"

Connor snorted. "No. She'd left her sweater in the restaurant and had gone back for it. By the time she came out, Todd was wearing a crocodile grin and the valet had pocketed a tip the size of his monthly paycheck."

Something else Dunworthy had in common with the Wilsons—thinking money could make anything or anyone disappear. Not that he blamed the kid for taking the cash. How could he when he'd done the same thing ten years ago?

"You don't think Todd would hurt Emily, do you?" Kelsey asked, disbelief and worry mingling in her expression.

"I don't know," he said. "All I know is that he thinks he can do whatever he damn well wants as long as he pays for the privilege."

"Kelsey! Where have you been all day?" Emily rose from the table in the middle of the Italian restaurant. "I've been calling you since first thing this morning."

Kelsey braced herself against Emily's exuberant greeting, hesitantly patting her cousin's slender shoulder blades. First thing this morning, Emily had been with Connor. Kelsey seriously doubted she'd been on her cousin's mind. "I've, um, been busy."

"What have you been doing?" Emily demanded as Kelsey slipped into a seat next to her and across from Aileen and her husband.

"I was—" Kelsey's mind blanked as she met her cousin's curious gaze, and she couldn't think of a single excuse.

I was with Connor. We spent the day spying on your fiancé, which was possibly the craziest thing I've ever done, right up to the time I thought Connor might kiss me.

"Kelsey!"

She jumped at the sound of her aunt's voice, terrified for a split second that she'd said the unbelievable words out loud. "What?"

Charlene frowned with a question in her eyes. "You paid the florist, didn't you?"

"Yes! Yes, I did." As if the forty-minute errand explained her absence during most of the day.

"Good. I hope it wasn't a mistake going with such a small shop. As worried as that woman sounded, you'd think she was down to her last dollar."

Irritation buzzed like a rash under Kelsey's skin. "Her name is Lisa Remming, and she's an amazing florist. A deposit is standard policy. We signed a contract stating she could cancel the order if it wasn't paid on time," she added, knowing her friend would never have considered canceling such an important order.

"All right, Kelsey. You've made your point," Charlene said. Kelsey thought she might have caught a hint of respect in her aunt's expression.

But Emily's eyes widened, and she grabbed Kelsey's hand. "Lisa wouldn't do that, would she?"

"No, of course not," she reassured her cousin, feeling like

a jerk for worrying her cousin just to make a point with Charlene. "The flowers are going to be beautiful."

Emily smiled, relieved someone else had solved the problem. "Thank goodness. I can't imagine getting married without the right bouquet."

Kelsey, personally, couldn't imagine getting married without the right groom. She *wanted* to believe Todd was that man for her cousin, but ever since Connor had rolled into town, doubts had swirled through her mind like a desert dust devil.

"Emily, darling!" a masculine voice called out. Dressed in designer slacks and a slate-blue silk shirt, Todd Dunworthy approached, his perfectly groomed blond hair glinting, and his teeth flashing in a blinding smile.

Sheep's clothing, Kelsey thought suddenly. Expensive, designer-crafted sheep's clothing…if she believed Connor. But that was the question. *Did* she believe him?

"Sorry I'm late," Todd apologized without looking away from his fiancée. "My meeting ran late."

"Your meeting?" Kelsey didn't realize she'd spoken the words out loud until all eyes turned her way. Tempted to blurt out that he'd spent less than five minutes at the office, she choked back the words. She couldn't say that without revealing her own presence. And, as she'd told Connor, Todd's meeting could have changed locations. Hoping Todd would reveal that was the case, she pressed, "I mean, what meeting, Todd?"

He waved his hand carelessly, and his sleeve pulled back to show a hint of the gold watch he wore. "Just business. You wouldn't be interested," he said, flashing a wink that was more condescending than charming.

"Oh, but I am," Kelsey interjected, when Todd would have changed the subject. He shot her a look clearly meant to back her down—*to put her in her place*—but Kelsey stood her ground. She could almost feel Connor at her back, giving her the strength to do the right thing. "You'll be family soon, and I hardly know anything about what you do."

"Honestly, Kelsey, enough about work," Emily interrupted, despite the fact that Todd had remained completely—suspiciously?—silent. "We have more important things to discuss."

Ever the peacemaker, Emily turned the conversation to the wedding and her honeymoon. She smoothed over the tension like a pro until, on the outside at least, everything *looked* perfect.

But as the conversation moved on to drinks and appetizers and who wanted to try the chef's special, Kelsey couldn't help noticing how her cousin's gaze would occasionally drift off in the distance. And she wondered if maybe, just maybe, Emily was waiting for Connor—or *anyone*—to rescue her again.

Connor drummed his fingers against the steering wheel, his gaze locked on the Italian restaurant. Candlelight flickered in the antique sconces, illuminating the rustic red brick, aged pergola, and carved wooden doors.

After taking Kelsey back to the hotel and her car, Connor called Jake Cameron, eager to hear what the man had found. But the conversation hadn't gone as he'd hoped.

"I told you this would take some time," Jake had said, sounding more frustrated and less confident than during the last call.

"Yeah, I know. You also told me you had a date with Sophia Pirelli. You had to have found *something.*"

Silence filled the line, and Connor might have thought the call was disconnected, except he could still sense his friend's tension coming across loud and clear. "Jake—"

"Look, I'm seeing her again. I'll call you later."

He'd hung up after that, leaving Connor to battle his own tension and frustration. Unwilling to sit in his hotel room and go over the same information on Dunworthy again, he'd headed for Todd's condo, planning to talk with some of the man's neighbors, when he spotted the familiar SUV leaving the parking garage.

As Connor followed Dunworthy from his Scottsdale loft, careful to stay two car lengths behind, he had plenty of time to make some calls, and discovered the studio-sized units cost well over two million dollars. Knowing the man would pay such an outrageous price for an exclusive address to call home, Connor should have expected what was to come.

He'd already trailed Emily's fiancé from one expensive store to another, growing more and more disgusted as Dunworthy racked up a small fortune in purchases. Wine shops, jewelers, tailors. Connor had held back far enough to keep Dunworthy from spotting him, but not so far that he couldn't see the dollar signs in the salespeople's eyes.

The afternoon had proved a dud just like the meeting that morning, and Connor wished Kelsey had come along. He missed her company—an odd admission for a man who worked alone. He missed her wry comments and witty comebacks, not to mention the tempting thought of kissing her. It was no longer a question of if, but when…

He did have one lead, thanks to a call he'd overheard Todd make on his cell phone, but he would have to wait to follow up.

He sat up straight in the driver's seat as the restaurant's carved doors opened. "'Bout time," he muttered as the elder Wilsons stepped outside along with Aileen and her husband. Todd and Emily followed, and even though Connor had his gaze locked on the other man, it didn't take much to distract him. Just Kelsey.

She stood apart from the rest of the group—not so far she couldn't hear the conversation, just far enough she couldn't be easily drawn in. He'd noticed her do that at the hotel when he'd crashed their little reception planning session. She'd trailed a step or two behind her aunt and cousin, hiding behind the copious notes she took in her day planner. Observing, but not really joining.

Just the way he did. He never would have thought his job as a private eye and Kelsey's job as a wedding coordinator would give them something else in common, but there it was. Still, the Wilsons were more than Kelsey's clients; they were her family. So what was the reason for that distance?

Now wasn't the time to worry about it. Connor jerked his gaze away from Kelsey. He didn't let his attention stray back to her, not even once, surprised by how hard that was.

Todd slapped his future father-in-law on the back, then kissed Charlene's cheek and said something to make the older woman laugh.

I'll be damned, Connor thought, his respect for Dunworthy as an adversary rising a few notches. He'd never seen the woman crack a smile, yet Todd had Emily's mother eating out of his hand.

The group, a silent film of family togetherness, said their goodbyes amid hugs and kisses, with Kelsey drifting just outside the happy circle. They broke into pairs, the elder Wilsons off to the left with Aileen and her husband, Emily and Dunworthy to his car—illegally parked, Connor noted—alongside the restaurant. Kelsey, the odd woman out, headed toward the back of the restaurant, crossing the parking lot…alone.

Todd's SUV engine roared. He should follow, Connor knew. His hand went to the ignition, but he didn't turn the key. A gut feeling, the kind Kelsey had sardonically discounted, held him in place even as Todd backed his vehicle away from the restaurant.

He had to go now if he had any hope of following. Instead, he leaned forward. Kelsey had nearly disappeared around the building. That side of the restaurant wasn't as well lit. Her hair looked brown in the meager light, the shadows dousing its fiery color. Dressed in a denim skirt and lace-trimmed green T-shirt, she looked smaller than usual…younger and more vulnerable.

Connor had already pushed the car door open before he caught sight of the dark shape of a man cutting across the parking lot and heading her way. Surprise drew Kelsey up short. Connor was still too far away to hear what she said, but he was close enough to see the guy reach out to grab her.

It was his nightmare brought to life. Close enough to see, too far away to help… For a split second, Connor froze until he realized this was no dream and the woman in danger wasn't Cara Mitchell. It was *Kelsey.*

Adrenaline pounded through his veins. A short burst of speed, the rhythmic thumping of feet against pavement, and he was there. Muscles flexing, he had the guy's arm twisted behind his back, his face shoved against the side of the restaurant.

"You okay?" he demanded of Kelsey, surprised by the breathless gasp fueling the words. His heart pounded like he'd run half a mile instead of thirty yards. Trying to outrun the past…

"Kelsey?" He could feel her behind him but didn't risk looking over his shoulder. "Are you okay?"

"Connor, what—" Too stunned by his sudden appearance to get the words out, Kelsey pressed a hand to her pounding heart, surprised the organ was still where it was supposed to be. For a second, she thought it had jumped right out of her chest.

"Did he hurt you?"

She blinked, the question not quite registering, and stared at her ex-boyfriend, who was pressed like a pancake against the restaurant's brick wall. Matt Moran had hurt her. He'd wounded her pride, trashed her self-confidence, hitting her where she was most vulnerable with the reminder she could never compare to her oh-so-beautiful cousin.

Matt made a strangled, high-pitched sound that might have been her name. "Kelsey! Tell him I wouldn't hurt you."

Connor shot her a quick glance. "You know this guy?"

The tension eased from his shoulders, but Kelsey knew he could be back in battle mode in a split second. The masculine display shouldn't have impressed her. She'd never advocated violence as a way to problem-solve. But seeing her former boyfriend pinned to a wall, well, it did her heart some good.

"Yes. You can let him go. He just wanted to talk to me."

Only, Kelsey hadn't wanted to hear anything Matt had to say. She'd already heard it all, ironically enough, from Connor.

He let go of the other man's arm and spun him around. "I take it you don't want to talk to him," Connor said. "Can't blame you there." He gave the other man a hard, intense look, then seemed to sum up Matt's entire character with a single shake of his head. Too bad Connor hadn't been around when Kelsey first met Matt.

Oh, who are you kidding? a mocking inner voice asked. She would never have noticed Matt if Connor had been around. But for all their differences, Connor and Matt had one glaring similarity.

"Kelsey, please," her ex-boyfriend practically whimpered. "You've gotta talk to Emily and tell her she can't marry that guy!"

Even without glancing in Connor's direction, she could feel his gaze. Heat rose to her face. She wanted to ignore both men at the moment, but she focused on Matt who was suddenly, oddly enough, the lesser of two humiliations.

"Emily's in love with Todd, and their wedding is going to be perfect." Determination rang in her voice, but Kelsey wondered who she was hoping to convince.

"You don't understand!" Matt took a single step in her direction, but froze when Connor uncrossed his arms. Keeping a nervous eye on the other man, Matt weakly finished, "I love her."

"Believe me. That is one thing I *do* understand."

He'd offered the same pitiful excuse as an explanation for using her, for taking advantage of her feelings, for making love to her and imagining Emily in her place.

Her ex-boyfriend had the grace to hang his head in shame but not enough sense to know when to give up. "Maybe if I could talk to her—" Matt pressed.

"Oh, for Pete's sake, get over it!"

His eyes widened in surprise, but Kelsey felt a shock when the words sank into her soul, and she realized the real object of her anger. She was tired of feeling like a fool for believing his lies. Of accepting his unacceptable behavior. Of shouldering the blame for the failure of their relationship when Matt was at fault.

"Let it go, Matt, and move on. I have."

Maybe that wasn't entirely true. As far as love was concerned, she certainly wasn't ready to take the plunge again, but might it be worthwhile to test the water?

"The lady asked you to leave." Connor crossed his arms over his broad chest, suddenly seeming to take up twice as much space and ready to literally enforce her advice for Matt to move on.

With a single, pitiful glance at Kelsey, Matt shrank back into the shadows. She didn't know if he'd heard a single word she said, but it didn't matter. *She'd* listened.

"Man, you've had your work cut out for you, haven't you?" Connor asked, once Matt had left. "How many of Emily's exes have you had to deal with?"

Emily's exes. Kelsey crossed her arms over her stomach, some of her earlier pleasure fading. The toe she'd stuck in the deep end felt chilled by frigid water. "So far, you're the only one. Matt isn't one of Emily's ex-boyfriends. He's mine."

Kelsey didn't know why she spilled that bit of information.

It wasn't as if she wanted Connor to feel sorry for her. She didn't know *what* she wanted from him.

He kicked at the asphalt and glanced in the direction the other man had disappeared. "Hell, Kelsey, you shoulda told me that before. I wouldn't have been so gentle."

The unexpected comment startled a laugh from her. It bubbled inside, shaky at first but growing stronger until she felt lighter, buoyed by the emotion and perhaps the chance to let go of the past. "How exactly do you throw a man *gently* against a wall?"

"*Gently* means he gets to slink off under his own power. *Not so gently* requires an ambulance."

"I guess Matt doesn't know how lucky he was."

"You're right, Kelsey. Something tells me he has no idea."

Certainty filled Connor's deep voice. Just listening to him made her feel free from the shame and embarrassment that had held her down for so long. Stepping closer, he crooked a finger beneath her chin. "You okay?"

She nodded, feeling his finger slide along the sensitive skin beneath her jaw. "Yes."

Concern gave way to relief and then anger. "You should have had someone walk you to your car. You have no idea what could happen—"

"Connor, I'm okay," Kelsey interrupted, worried by the tension that was evident in the set of his shoulders. A tension that seemed rooted in a different incident from a different time. "I wasn't in any danger."

Exhaling a breath, Connor seemed to release the pressure building inside and shake off whatever memories had caught him in their grasp. "You still need to be more careful."

True, Matt had startled her, coming out of the shadows the way he had, but he'd lost the power to hurt her long ago. And despite Connor's warning that she should be more careful, *he* was the most dangerous threat around. His lethal charm tore through her defenses, and a question that should have come to her much, much sooner sprang to mind. "What are *you* doing here, anyway? How did you even know we'd be having dinner tonight?"

Connor glanced at the front of the restaurant. A frown darkened his expression before he shook his head and blew out a breath. "Well, I *was* following Todd."

"What!"

"That's how I knew he was at the restaurant," he explained slowly, as if she had trouble keeping up. "So, tell me about dinner."

"Not so fast. You first."

"Okay," he said agreeably. "I haven't had dinner yet, and I'm starving!"

"I meant, tell me what you found following Todd."

"I will, but I really am starving. Come on." With a last look at the now-empty spot in front of the restaurant, he caught Kelsey's hand and said, "Let's go."

"Go where?" she demanded even as she followed alongside, far too aware of the tingle that raced up her spine as his fingers entwined with hers. The innocent touch certainly shouldn't have weakened her knees, but Kelsey could barely concentrate beyond the heat of his skin pressed to hers.

"To find someplace to eat."

Despite the extreme heat during the day, the temperature had lowered with the sunset. A gentle breeze carried the scents and sounds of nearby shops: gourmet coffee, decadent chocolate, the rise and fall of laughter and the faint strains of jazz music.

A group of girls walked toward Kelsey and Connor, heading in the other direction. Tall and beautiful, long limbs left bare by short skirts and tank tops, their not-so-subtle glances at Connor quickly turned to confusion as they shifted to Kelsey.

She didn't need a thought bubble over their heads to know what they were thinking: *What is* he *doing with* her? And after the run-in with Matt, Kelsey couldn't stop that question from digging deeper and deeper.

"Hey." Connor tugged at her hand. "You still with me?" he asked, as if he had somehow lost *her* interest.

"I'm here," she said. Now if she could only focus on *why* she was there. "Did you find anything on Todd?"

Connor took his time answering, waiting until he'd found a casual dining restaurant with outdoor seating. Cooling misters hissed overhead, the sound blending with the distant strains of an acoustic guitar being played on an outdoor stage. After giving the waiter his order, Connor leaned back in his chair and said, "If I'd found anything, you'd be the first to know. Unfortunately, all he did was shop."

"All afternoon?"

He laughed at her startled response. "I thought you'd be impressed."

"Surprised is more like it," she muttered, thinking of Todd's excuse. Still, she hesitated before confessing, "Todd was late for dinner. He said it was because of a business meeting."

"What? That five-second trip to his office this morning?" Connor scoffed.

"Maybe he didn't want to tell Emily he'd gone shopping for her."

"Except he was shopping for himself—unless Emily's taken up imported cigars."

"Um, no."

After a waiter dropped off glasses of ice water and Connor's steak sandwich, he said, "What else?"

"It was dinner, Connor, not an inquisition," she said as Connor dug in with both hands.

Truthfully, Kelsey hadn't *wanted* to find anything. She

wanted to believe Todd and Emily would have a beautiful wedding followed by a happy marriage. "It's probably nothing but—" she paused, not believing her own words "—none of Todd's family are coming to the wedding."

"Did he say why?" he asked, sliding his plate of fries her way.

Kelsey shook her head at the offer and said, "His parents already had a trip to Europe planned, and his sister is pregnant and didn't want to travel."

Connor shrugged. "So it could be nothing."

She blinked. Connor had jumped on even the slightest inconsistency in Todd's behavior. She couldn't believe he was letting this one go. "Are you serious? Can you imagine my aunt and uncle *not* showing up to Emily's wedding?"

"Not every family is like yours."

"Okay, fine. Forget the Wilsons. You might be the P.I. expert, but I'm the wedding expert, remember? And families *always* come to weddings!"

Connor's gaze cut away from her as he balled a paper napkin between his fists, and Kelsey knew. This wasn't about Todd's family or her family or families in general. It was about Connor's. A family she knew nothing about, one she couldn't recall Emily ever mentioning.

"You know, I don't think Emily's ever talked about your family."

"Why would she?"

Because, at one time or another, Emily had told Kelsey nearly everything about Connor. So much that Kelsey felt she'd known him long before she first caught sight of him at the airport. But she certainly couldn't tell Connor how she'd listened to those stories the same way a teenager might pore over celebrity magazines for the latest gossip on the current Hollywood heartthrob.

"I don't know. Maybe because if things had worked out like you'd planned, they would have been *her* family, too."

Connor gave a rough bark of laughter. "Emily had enough family to deal with without adding mine to the mix. Besides, my parents died before I met Emily."

The abrupt comment hit Kelsey in the chest, and she felt ashamed for pushing. She ached for his loss, an echo to the pain she still felt over the death of her own mother.

"Oh, Connor." Her defenses crumbled to dust, and with her heart already reaching out, her hands immediately followed. The heat of his hands—strong, rawboned, and masculine—sent an instant jolt up her arms. Her heart skipped a beat at the simple contact, but it was the emotional connection that had her pulse picking up an even greater speed. For a second, as their eyes met, Connor looked as startled as she felt.

Taking a breath deep enough to force her heart back into place, she focused on the reason she'd dared touch him in the first place. "I'm so sorry. I lost my mom when I was sixteen. Do you want—"

"It was a long time ago," he interrupted, jerking his hands out from hers in a pretense of reaching for his wallet to pull out a few bills. "I should get going. I'll walk you back to your car."

Stung by his abrupt withdrawal, Kelsey ducked her head before he could see the embarrassed color burning in her cheeks. Focusing on her purse, she searched for the keys she knew perfectly well were in the outside pocket.

"No need. I'll be fine," she insisted, and started walking. But if she thought she could out-stubborn Connor, he quickly proved her wrong.

"You will be fine," he agreed, his light touch against her lower back a complete contrast to the steely determination in his voice. "Because I'm walking you to your car."

Kelsey didn't argue, even though Matt was probably long gone. Thanks to Connor, he'd learned his lesson. Too bad she had yet to learn hers. Because no matter what Connor said about how beautiful she was, actions spoke louder than words, and all the compliments in the world couldn't erase the hurt of reaching out to Connor only to have him pull away.

Chapter Six

Early the next morning Kelsey stood outside her shop, gripping the key tightly enough to dig grooves into her palm. The unexpected phone call from her landlord couldn't have come at a better time. She still had plenty left to do for Emily's wedding, but she couldn't think of Emily without thinking of Connor. And Kelsey definitely did *not* want to think of him. Last night, she'd felt a connection—that loss and difficult childhoods gave them something in common. But Connor didn't want common.

He didn't want *her*.

With the morning sunlight glinting off the windows, she couldn't see inside, but in her mind's eye she pictured *her* shop. The subtle green and pink colors, the faded rose wall-paper, the shabby-chic-style parlor where she would meet with clients. Romantic without being overblown; classy while still being casual.

It was going to be perfect. Excitement jazzing her veins, Kelsey stuck the key in the lock, opened the door and blinked. With her dream office so firm in her thoughts she could practically smell her favorite peach potpourri, reality hit like a slap to the forehead.

No soft colors, no floral wallpaper… Shabby, yes, but chic?

"Not even close," Kelsey muttered as she flicked on the lights and stepped inside.

The landlord had shown her the space a few weeks ago, when it had been a struggling craft store. Shelves and bins had lined every wall, filled with yarn and cloth, paints and silk flowers. She'd focused on the space, knowing everything else would go when the other store closed. But she never stopped to think about the mess left behind.

Holes from the now-absent shelves marred the walls with peg-board consistency. The carpet had a two-tone hue thanks to the areas exposed to foot traffic, and the bare fluorescent bulbs overhead buzzed like bug zappers in August. No wonder the landlord had left the key hidden outside instead of meeting Kelsey.

But Kelsey hadn't spent her childhood living in sub-par apartments without learning a thing or two from her mother. "Wilson women against the world," she murmured as she pulled the phone from her purse and called the landlord.

If there was one thing Connor hated, it was being wrong. The only thing worse was being wrong and knowing he had to apologize. Meeting his own gaze in the mirror, he knew he owed Kelsey a big apology. He'd seen the hurt in her chocolate eyes at his abrupt withdrawal and he felt like a jerk. She'd reached out to him—physically and emotionally—and he'd pulled away.

He could justify his actions with the same excuse he always used when thoughts of the past intruded. That time was over and done, enough said. And yet, the sympathy and understanding in Kelsey's expression made him *want* to talk about the past. He'd wanted to turn his wrist, take her hand into his and hold on tight. That completely foreign desire had so rattled him, that he'd locked his jaw and put an early end to the evening.

After showering and throwing on some clothes, Connor called Kelsey's cell. The phone rang four times before she answered, sounding breathless and sexy and— "Where the hell are you?" he demanded before he could keep the words from bursting out.

And what was she *doing* to give her voice that husky, bedroom quality?

"I'm…working."

She was *lying.* Before he could remind himself what Kelsey did or who she did it with was none of his business, he heard a loud clatter followed by an abbreviated scream and a thump that sent his heart racing. "Kelsey!" Silence filled the line, giving Connor plenty of time to imagine half a dozen dangerous possibilities. "Kelsey!"

"I'm here. I'm fine," she said after what sounded like a scramble for the phone. "I knocked over a ladder and a bucket of spackle went flying."

Ladder? "Spackle?"

"You know," she said, her voice sounding slightly muffled, and he imagined the phone held against her shoulder. "That compound stuff you use to patch walls."

"I know what spackle is. The big question is, why do *you* know what it is?"

"I'm just handy that way," she said a little too brightly, and Connor flashed back to the hurt in her eyes. Her answer might have been different if he hadn't pulled away the night before. "Kelsey—"

"I've found an office space to rent. That way I'll have more room to sell my lies about happily-ever-after to unsuspecting brides and grooms."

Connor flinched despite her light-hearted tone. Seemed as if he might have even more to apologize for than he'd thought. "What's the address?"

"Why?" she asked, as if she thought he planned to come by and torch the place.

"Because," he said after a deep breath and a ten count for patience, "I owe you an apology." Kelsey didn't respond, and in the silence, Connor knew she wanted more. That need rose up again, pressure building inside him as words he'd held back for years struggled to get out. "I owe you an apology," he repeated, "and an explanation."

"I'm an idiot," Kelsey muttered as she washed spackle from her hands in the tiny bathroom. She would have liked to look herself in the eye as she spoke those words, but the bathroom was missing a mirror, had no hot water, and a questionable-at-best toilet.

Why had she given Connor the address? Why had she invited him to invade her place? The dream office that filled her thoughts so strongly that morning had faded over the past several hours of hard work. The last thing she needed was Connor's presence to overwhelm what was left of her lace-and-roses dream in a deluge of cotton and denim.

Not to mention his cynicism.

Yet she'd been unable to resist the demand in his voice or his promised apology.

The ring of the bell above the front door alerted her to her first visitor and saved her from her own thoughts. "Kelsey?" a familiar female voice called out.

She banged on the faucet handle a few times to turn off the

water and hurried out, shaking her hands to get them dry. "Lisa? What are you doing here?"

Walking through the shop with a bouquet of gerbera daisies in one hand and a bottle of wine in the other, her friend cast a dubious look around. "Not quite what I expected," she said as she met Kelsey at the back of the shop.

"It needs work," Kelsey admitted. "But I called the landlord and talked him into reducing the first month's rent if I handle the repairs."

"And that's why I'm here," her friend announced as she set the wine and flowers on the ladder. "I know you too well. You're always willing to help your friends, but you never ask for help. Of course, I had no idea you'd need this much help, but it's a good thing I called Trey, too." Trey Jamison was another good friend, and she frequently hired him as a DJ for her weddings.

"You didn't have to do that," Kelsey told Lisa.

"Yes, I did because you wouldn't. I knew you'd be here all alone with no one to help you and…"

Lisa turned as the bell announced another arrival, her words trailing away. Kelsey couldn't blame her friend. She felt pretty speechless as Connor stripped off his reflective glasses and locked that green gaze on her from across the shop. "Hey."

"Hey," Kelsey responded, the word far more breathless than she wanted to admit. Her stomach did a slow roll at the sight of him. Just as she'd feared, he shrank the space until it encompassed only the two of them. Thoughts of lace and roses fell away, overwhelmed by Connor's masculine presence. Her senses took in every bit of him—the faded gray T-shirt that stretched across his chest, the jeans that clung to his muscular legs, the low murmur of his voice.

Lisa's silence didn't last nearly as long as Kelsey's. Her friend gripped her arm and whispered, "Who *is* that?"

"Connor McClane," Kelsey murmured back.

"Connor—" Lisa's eyebrows rose. "Emily's ex? What is he doing here?"

Emily's ex. Kelsey's heart cringed at the description. "Good question," she muttered as his promised apology and explanation rang in her mind.

Before she had the chance to ask, Trey pushed through the doorway. With his long hair caught back in a ponytail, and wearing an oversize T-shirt and raggedy cutoffs, he looked ready to work. But after gazing around, he said, "Way to go, Kelse!" Walking over, he spun her in an exuberant hug. "This place is great."

"You think?" she asked, with a laugh at her friend's enthusiasm.

"Well, it will be when you're done with it, right?" He glanced at Lisa and Connor for confirmation, and only then did Kelsey realize she had yet to introduce them.

"Oh, I'm sorry. Trey, Lisa, this is Connor…"

The introduction faded away as she caught sight of the scowl on Connor's face. Instinctively she stepped out of Trey's embrace, which was *crazy.* Because Trey was just a friend and crazier still because Connor could *not* be jealous.

Could he?

Still, Connor was less than friendly as he crossed the shop to greet Trey. The handshake the two men exchanged seemed more like a prelude to battle than a customary introduction. "Good to meet you," Trey said, his smile growing wide even though Kelsey thought she saw him subtly flexing his hand once Connor released it.

"Pleasure," Connor said, the word sounding anything but.

"Okay, let's put all this testosterone to use," Lisa said, bringing a heated blush to Kelsey's face. "Where do we start?"

"Yeah, give us the list," Trey said, holding out his hand.

"You guys don't have to do this. You can't give up your weekend to help me out."

"Like the time you filled in for me when I got snowed in back East and didn't have anyone to open up the flower shop?" Lisa challenged before glancing at Trey expectantly.

Immediately he picked up where she'd left off. "Or the time you shoved chicken soup and hot tea down my throat to get my voice back in time to DJ that last wedding?"

"That's different," Kelsey protested.

"Why? Why are you the only one allowed to help?" Lisa demanded. "When do we get to return the favor? And hey, we're not dummies. We all know helping you helps us."

"Yeah, as long as she doesn't forget her friends when she's off coordinating weddings for the rich and famous," Trey whispered in an aside to Lisa.

Overwhelmed by their generosity, Kelsey blinked back tears. Growing up, it had always been Kelsey and her mom—Wilson women against the world. But maybe that was only because Olivia hadn't had friends as amazing as Lisa and Trey.

"All right! All right! I give in. And I promise to remember all the little people," Kelsey laughed before grabbing the list as well as a handful of paint swatches, wallpaper samples and various store ads from her day planner.

"Trey, here are the paint colors and wallpaper. If you could pick them up from the hardware store along with a carpet steamer, that would be great. Lisa, here's a picture of the drapes I want for the front window. Could you see if they have a large area rug to match? Anything to hide this carpet."

Even as Kelsey split the shopping between her friends, she was aware of Connor's speculative gaze focused on her. What was he thinking? she wondered. That her romantic trappings were literally that—traps for couples foolish enough to believe in love?

"Got it, boss," Trey said, saluting her with the green and pink paint samples. "Want me to pick up lunch while I'm out?"

"No need. Sara's catering our workday. Her word, not mine," Lisa laughed as she grabbed Trey's arm and led him toward the door.

"Man, I wanted pizza and beer. Sara'll probably bring mini quiches and crudités." As the two of them walked outside, the laughter and casual camaraderie went with them, leaving behind a tension that for Kelsey buzzed as loudly as the fluorescent light overhead.

Ready to take the offensive, she turned to Connor. What apology did he want to give? What explanation? Her lips parted on those questions, but he beat her to the punch.

"How many of your friends are working Emily's wedding?"

Just like that, momentum changed, and Connor had her backpedaling and on the defensive. "Lisa and I went to high school together, and I've made friends with some of the other people I've worked with. But I never would have hired them if I didn't think they'd do an awesome job."

She lifted her chin, ready to battle for her friends the same way she had when she hired them for Emily's wedding. But if this was a fight, Connor didn't play fair.

Reaching up, he tucked a loose curl behind one ear. His eyes glowing with a warmth that stole the fight from her spirit and the breath from her lungs, he murmured, "It wasn't a criticism. Only an observation. Your friends obviously care a lot about you. Just like you care about them."

Intensity lit his emerald eyes, and Kelsey could almost believe he wanted her to look out for him, to care about him—but that had to be a delusion due to lack of oxygen from the breath he'd stolen with his nearness. "I do," she managed to murmur.

"So why was it so hard for you to accept their help?"

She started to deny it, but when Connor's eyebrows rose

in challenge, she knew he wouldn't believe anything but the truth. And maybe if she told him, he would understand why Emily's wedding was so important. "Fixing things is what I do. It's what I'm good at. I wasn't brought up as one of the wealthy Wilsons. I was raised by my mother. We didn't have much, but growing up I didn't know that. All I knew was that I had an amazing mother who taught me how to cook delicious meals without spending more than a few dollars and how to clip coupons to make the most of what little money we had."

A memory came to mind, and Kelsey smiled. "Our favorite day was Black Friday, but we didn't just shop for Christmas. We bargain-hunted for the whole year. My mom taught me how to look at secondhand furniture and see beyond the layers of flaking paint or rust. She showed me how to strip away the exterior to the natural beauty beneath."

Her smile faded away. "But then she died, and I came to live with my aunt and uncle. None of the things I knew how to do mattered anymore. Coupons and discount stores and secondhand furniture were as foreign to them as paying hundreds of dollars for a pair of shoes was to me. They had people to shop and clean and fix things." Kelsey gave a short, sad laugh. "The only thing broken in their house was me. I know they cared about me, but...I just didn't fit, no matter how hard I tried."

"Kelsey." The low murmur of Connor's voice mirrored the tenderness in his gaze. This time it was Kelsey's turn to pull away, to try to escape.

"That's why the wedding is so important. It's my chance—" her *only* chance, because if she screwed this up, why would the Wilsons or anyone trust her again? "—to prove that I can do this, that I'm good at *something.* So I really hope your gut's wrong, Connor, and that Todd is everything my family thinks he is. Or all this hard work is going to be for nothing."

"It won't be for nothing because you're going to be a

success with or without Emily's wedding. Maybe if you *were* more like Emily or Aileen, more used to everything going your way, you'd be more likely to give up. But a single setback won't stop you. You're stronger than that." Catching her hands and smiling at the streaks of spackle marring her skin, he said, "You aren't afraid of hard work."

Strong…unafraid… Kelsey liked the sound of that, but she wasn't feeling the least bit of either as Connor stroked his thumbs across the palm of her hands. She felt downright weak and terrified by the desire coursing through her at such a simple touch.

Her fingertips tingled, tempted to chart the planes and angles of his face, the strong column of his throat. The broad shoulders and wide chest covered by cotton as soft as Connor's body was strong. But she curled her hands into fists. She wouldn't—couldn't—reach out to him again. The embarrassment of Connor pulling away was too painfully fresh in her mind, and her heart was too vulnerable to risk rejection a second time.

In the end, she didn't have to reach out; she didn't even have to move. It was Connor who pulled her closer, Connor who lowered his head, Connor who brushed his mouth against hers. Any thought of him pulling away disappeared as he deepened the kiss. He buried one hand in her hair and wrapped the other around her waist, holding her body tight to his, as if she were the one who might back away.

But escape was the last thing Kelsey wanted.

Instead she wanted to capture this moment, bottle it up, save it for a time when memories were all she would have left of Connor. But even that proved impossible, as he slanted his mouth over hers, his lips and tongue stealing her breath, robbing her of her ability to think, and leaving her with no choice but to feel….

Her breasts against the hard wall of his chest, her heart pounding desperately enough to match the rapid beat of his, the firm press of his fingers against her hip. She splayed her fingers across his back, searching out as much contact as possible, the material thin enough, soft enough, heated enough, that she could imagine his naked skin and the play of muscles beneath her hands.

"Connor." His name escaped her on a breathless sigh as he trailed a kiss across her cheek to her jaw, his warm breath setting off a chain reaction of shivers down her spine. She swayed closer, her hips brushing against his solid thigh. The heated contact weakened her knees, and all she wanted was to sink to the floor, pull Connor down with her and feel the weight of his body on top of hers.

She might have done just that if not for the ring of the bell and an embarrassed "Oops. Pretend I was never here."

Kelsey tore away from Connor in time to see her friend Sara backing out of the door with a platter of food in her hands. She wanted to call Sara back, but it was too late, leaving Kelsey with little choice but to face Connor. With his eyes dark with passion, his chest rising and falling, it was all she could do not to dive back into his arms.

Two seconds ago an interruption was the last thing she wanted. But now with passion clearing, she realized it was exactly what she needed. Already Connor was going to her head; it wouldn't take much for him to go straight to her heart. "That, um, was Sara. I should ask her to come back inside."

Her friends were waiting, her dreams were waiting and she didn't dare push them aside. Not even for Connor. No matter how much she wanted to.

Hours later, Connor looked around Kelsey's shop, amazed by the transformation. The scent of paint filled the shop, and the soft pink and green colors highlighted the walls. The carpets had been shampooed, and the new rug and drapes stored in the back would soon complete the new look. Kelsey's self-proclaimed talent for stripping away the layers and revealing the beauty beneath was on magnificent display in all the work she'd done.

How could she possibly doubt her own worth, her own ability? Connor wondered…until he tried to imagine Emily—or heaven forbid, Charlene—dressed in a T-shirt and cutoffs, with their hair covered by a bandana, a streak of pale pink war paint on one cheek and spackle on the other. None of the other Wilson women would be caught dead looking the way Kelsey did right then. Yet seeing her eyes sparkle as she laughed with her friends, celebrated every small success and worked her *ass* off, Connor didn't think he'd ever seen a woman look as vibrant, as alive, as *sexy,* as Kelsey.

As if feeling the heat of his gaze, Kelsey glanced his way. Heat flared in her cheeks, and she ducked her head, taking a sudden interest in flipping through the phone directory, cell phone in hand as she searched for a plumber.

A phone call to her uncle, and her plumbing problems would have been solved. Hell, a single call to Gordon Wilson and *all* her problems would have been solved. Gordon could have easily set up Kelsey in a furnished, upscale Scottsdale or Paradise Valley suite instead of a work-in-progress strip mall in downtown Glendale.

He'd meant every word when he called Kelsey strong and fearless. She'd been only sixteen when she went to live with her aunt and uncle, an age when most kids would have lost themselves in a world filled with wealth and privilege. But not Kelsey. She'd stayed true to herself, to the lessons her mother had taught her. Even now, when her family's money could make her dream an instant success, Kelsey refused to take the easy way out…not like he had.

He'd had his reasons for taking the money Gordon Wilson had offered him to leave town all those years ago, reasons he believed justified his actions, but he couldn't help thinking that had Kelsey faced the same choice, she would have found another way.

She flat-out amazed him. He would have liked to ignore the emotion spilling through him, but Connor had learned his lesson when it came to ignoring feelings…even if this one wasn't hitting his gut as much as it was pulling at his heart.

"Place looks great, doesn't it?"

The sudden question jerked Connor from his thoughts, and he turned to face Lisa. Judging by the woman's sharp gaze, he doubted Kelsey's shop was on the woman's mind. "It does. You, Trey and Sara were a huge help," he added.

Kelsey's friends had thrown themselves into helping, Trey especially. But despite the close eye Connor kept on the other man, he hadn't seen any proof Trey and Kelsey were anything other than friends. And yet Trey's touchy-feely familiarity had set Connor's teeth on edge. A reaction as unfamiliar as it was uncomfortable.

He rarely felt possessive over a woman, and certainly not after a kiss or two. But then again, what a kiss! He could still taste her, could smell the cinnamon and spice he'd come to associate with Kelsey. No too-sweet floral scents for her. Nothing expensive, nothing fancy, just…Kelsey.

"You weren't too bad yourself," Lisa said with enough tongue-in-cheek attitude to make Connor wonder if she'd noticed how he strove to outlift, outwork, out*do* Trey. Turning serious, she said, "We're all glad to help Kelsey. She's the kind of friend who always takes care of everyone else. This is the first chance we've had to pay her back."

"I doubt she expects payment."

"She doesn't. It's in her nature to help." The brunette paused, and Connor sensed her debating over her next words. "I think a lot of it comes from taking care of her mom."

"Kelsey told me her mother died when she was sixteen." But despite what she'd told him, Connor knew he had only part of the story. Why had Kelsey's mother—Gordon Wilson's sister—raised Kelsey on her own? Single mom or not, she should have had the family fortune at her disposal, and yet that clearly hadn't been the case.

What had caused the rift between Kelsey's mother and her family? And what about the father Kelsey never mentioned? Connor didn't ask Lisa those questions. It was up to Kelsey to offer answers…if he asked her.

With a glance at her watch, Lisa told him she had to go, but she left with a few final words he translated into a warning. "Kelsey's a great girl. She deserves the best."

Connor waited for the woman to add that Kelsey deserved better than him, but when she merely gazed at him in expectation, he realized Lisa wasn't telling him Kelsey deserved better *than him;* she was telling him Kelsey deserved the best *from him.*

"Well, I finally found a plumber who can come this week…" Kelsey's voice trailed off as she walked from the back room, cell phone in hand.

Connor stood alone in the middle of the shop. Even with the progress they'd made, bringing her dream closer to reality, he overwhelmed the place. If anything, the shop's increasingly feminine decor only served as a larger reminder of Connor's masculinity. And after that kiss, Kelsey didn't have any doubt whatsoever about his undeniable and—she was beginning to fear—irresistible masculinity.

"Lisa had to take off," he explained.

"Oh. She was probably afraid I'd put her to work again if she didn't sneak away."

"I don't think so. Your friends will obviously do anything for you."

Uncomfortable with the praise, Kelsey countered, "Like Javy would for you."

Connor frowned. "Yeah. He thinks he owes me, but the truth is, his family bailed me out when I was a kid. Nothing I've done would be enough to repay them."

Despite the explanation he'd promised earlier, Connor's voluntary statement caught Kelsey off guard, surprising her almost as much as his kiss. She shook her head and protested, "Just because I spilled my guts doesn't mean you have to—"

"I want to," he interrupted. "I should have told you about my past last night, but I haven't told anyone since Señora Delgado pried it out of me as a kid."

"You—you didn't tell *anyone?*" Kelsey prodded.

You didn't tell Emily?

His penetrating gaze read into the heart of her question, hearing what she *hadn't* asked, and he vowed, "I didn't tell anyone."

And suddenly Kelsey wasn't sure she wanted to know. Listening to what he had to say seemed to take on a greater significance because Connor wanted to tell *her,* to confide in her, something he'd never told Emily.

Without saying another word, Connor stepped forward, his long strides erasing the distance between them. He caught her hand and led her over to the love seat her friends had surprised her with. She'd been overwhelmed by their generosity. The sofa would be the perfect place for her soon-to-be-married couples to sit side by side and decide floral arrangements, wedding invitations, dinner menus.

But as soon as Connor sank down onto the love seat, she

decided it would be the perfect place for her to curl up in his arms, the perfect place to kiss him and never stop. The masculine-feminine contrast sent a slow roll of awareness through her stomach as he settled back against the rose-covered cushions. In faded cotton and rough worn denim, he should have looked out of place; instead, his broad shoulders and wide chest looked far more comfortable and inviting than the floral chintz ever could.

Swallowing, she folded onto the couch beside him, one leg bent and angled toward Connor. He stared straight ahead, keeping his silence, and Kelsey sensed his thoughts drifting back to a past he'd purposely chosen not to face…until now.

Taking a deep breath, he said, "My father was a truck driver. Eighteen-wheeler. He worked hard, drank hard. He was…strict."

The tension in Connor's shoulders and the way his hands tightened into fists gave a clear definition of the word. Her heart ached for the boy he'd been, a boy she could picture so easily. Dark hair that was too long, a body that was too skinny, and a gaze that was too old. She could see him in her mind as if, somehow, he'd been there all along.

Crazy, she thought, but she felt she knew him so well. And now that Connor was willing to give out answers, did she dare ask more questions? Could she risk getting to know him even better?

In the end, no matter the potential danger to her heart, Kelsey had to ask. Not because she needed to hear the story… but because Connor needed to tell it. "And your mother?" she asked softly.

One by one his fingers unclenched then slowly laced together as if cradling something precious. "She was a dreamer. She was always…looking for something. Always hoping for a better life, only she never found it. I was eight when she died.

She'd been taking art lessons, or maybe it was a dance class. I can't remember."

Connor cleared his throat. "Anyway, this place wasn't in the best part of town. I begged her not to go. I knew something bad was going to happen. But she went anyway. No one knows exactly what happened," he added, the tension pulling at his shoulders revealing how much not knowing still troubled him, "but the police figured a mugging went wrong. Either my mom fought back or the guy panicked, and the gun went off."

"Oh, Connor, I'm so sorry." Just as she feared, her heart ached a little more at the telling, and she longed to reach out to him, to comfort him. But she didn't. This time it was her turn to twist her fingers together, strangling the desire to touch him.

Because—despite his kiss—she still feared her touch wasn't the one Connor wanted.

But he never told Emily about his family. He's telling you! Aching or not, her heart had the strength to argue, and Kelsey felt her resistance crumbling.

"The guy stole her purse and wallet," Connor went on as if she hadn't spoken. "It took three days before the police figured out who she was."

"Didn't your dad report her missing?"

"He was on a long-distance drive. He didn't know anything was wrong."

"But when your mother didn't come home, someone must have tried to get hold of him. The people you were staying with—" As soon as she said the words, realization flooded Kelsey and her breath caught. "You were alone, weren't you?"

"My mom thought I was old enough to take care of myself, and it should have only been for a few hours."

Hours that had stretched into days.

"Wasn't there anyone you could call? A friend of the family?"

"Probably, but hell, I was eight. My mom had told me she

was going to be right back. Calling someone would have been like admitting something was wrong, admitting she wasn't coming back. Ever."

Kelsey felt heartsick at the thought of the frightened, abandoned boy Connor had been. "You were so young. How did you get on without her?"

"My dad and I stumbled along, but he always blamed my mom for dying. If she'd been happy with her life, if she hadn't always been out looking for more and expecting something better, she'd still be alive. If she'd just *listened* to me. I could have—"

Saved her. Connor didn't say the words, but they rang in the silence and underscored everything he did. "It's not your fault, Connor," she insisted, and this time she couldn't keep from reaching out and grasping his hands as if she could somehow heal the pain and guilt with her touch. "People make their own decisions, and you aren't responsible for their choices."

"No, only for my own," he agreed darkly, but tension tightened his hands into rock-hard fists.

Her family was so wrong about Connor. He wasn't out to ruin Emily's wedding—he was trying to save her from a past he couldn't possibly change. But Kelsey still wasn't convinced Todd was the threat Connor thought him to be. After all, Connor's *gut reaction* had pinned Matt to the restaurant, mistakenly seeing her ex-boyfriend as a physical threat. Wasn't it possible Todd was as harmless as Matt, and Connor was looking through the eyes of the past and seeing a danger that wasn't there?

"I can't imagine what that must have been like to lose your mother so suddenly." *So violently.* "But don't you think maybe that's colored the way you see people?"

"People like Dunworthy?" he asked with a wry twist to his lips. He pulled his hands out from beneath hers in the pretense of shifting to face her on the love seat. "I know you think I'm wrong about him, but it's because of my past that I'm sure I'm right." As if sensing her doubt, he asked, "Haven't you ever met someone and instantly known the kind of person they are?"

Thoughts of her first impression of Connor assailed Kelsey. The bad boy. The troublemaker. The man out to ruin Emily's wedding and destroy Kelsey's chance to prove herself to her family, to make her mother proud… But he was so much more than that.

"Maybe once or twice."

"Like when you met me?"

One corner of his mouth kicked up with the teasing comment, but the smile lacked full-force charm, his heart not in it. The emotional waters had gotten too deep, and Connor was clearly pulling back to shallower depths. And Kelsey almost wished she had stayed on the surface, wished she could still see Connor the way he wanted to be seen—cocky, self-confident, unbreakable. But she felt herself going under, caught by the pull of this man who was so much more than the rebel he played.

Struggling to break free, she focused on the easy out Connor had taken and followed him to more solid ground. "I knew you were going to be trouble the moment I met you. Does that count?"

"Talk about biased," he murmured. "How many Connor McClane stories have you heard over the years?"

"More than a few."

"More than a few hundred, if your aunt and uncle had anything to say about it." The teasing tone stayed in his voice, but Kelsey could tell her family's poor opinion of him still rankled. He was clearly out to prove the Wilsons wrong, but Kelsey suspected he had as much to prove to himself. "And here I've been a perfect gentleman."

"Well, not perfect," she argued. But who wanted perfect? Perfect was for women like her cousins; Kelsey much preferred the real thing to Ken-like perfection.

"I'm crushed. Señora Delgado will be so disappointed."

"Señora Delgado?"

"Javy's mother."

"How did you and Javy meet?"

"We went to school together. Mrs. Brown's sixth-grade glass."

"And you two became fast friends?"

"Nah, we hated each other. I can't even remember why. Oh, wait, it had something to do with a girl. We thought we were pretty hot stuff on the playground. Both trying to impress Alicia Martin. Unfortunately for us, she had a thing for older men."

"Eighth grader?" Kelsey guessed, playing along to maintain the teasing mood.

"Worse. P.E. teacher. And man, the guy was old. Like twenty-five. Anyway, we bonded over a couple of cafeteria juice boxes, and I started hanging out with him at his mother's restaurant. Before long, I was washing dishes and bussing tables. If the Delgados hadn't fed me through most of junior high and high school, I don't know what I would have done. Probably would have dropped out to work full-time if Maria hadn't stopped me."

Kelsey knew the drop-out rate was horrible, especially in Arizona, but as much as she'd hated school, she never once considered not finishing. "How did she stop you?"

"By telling me I *should,*" Connor said wryly. "She said anyone foolish enough to give up a free education didn't deserve one."

Smiling at the woman's use of reverse psychology, Kelsey said, "I think I'd like to meet her. Not every woman has enough influence to keep a boy in school *and* teach him to clear dishes off a table."

"You're on. Let's go to the Delgados' restaurant. Maybe Maria will be there."

Kelsey swallowed. Was Connor asking her out? On a *date?* She waited for the little voice in her head to tell her this was a bad idea, but she didn't hear it. Possibly because it was drowned out by the *big* voice screaming, "Go for it!"

She knew the voice of reason would be back, loud and clear, and ready to say "I told you so" if she let herself fall for Connor. But that worry, like the voice, seemed far off, and she couldn't resist the chance to spend more time with Connor.

"I'm a mess," she said in weak protest. "I can't go anywhere looking like this."

As Connor's gaze swept over her, Kelsey felt her face heat. She could only imagine what he saw. She had spackle under her nails, drywall dust in her hair, and more splotches of paint than freckles covering her arms. She was sweaty and disheveled, and even though Connor had worked as hard as anyone, he looked—

Gorgeous, she thought with a sigh, taking in the lock of dark hair he'd constantly pushed back from his paint-streaked forehead, the hint of five o'clock shadow shading his jaw, the damp T-shirt that molded to his shoulders and chest.

"I'll pick you up at your place in half an hour," he said as he stood and reached down to pull her to her feet.

Kelsey shook her head, ready to refuse, and yet when she opened her mouth she said, "An hour."

"Forty-five minutes."

"An hour." She laughed as she shoved him toward the door. "And not a minute sooner."

Chapter Seven

Mariachi music greeted Connor as he opened the car door. Judging by the nearly full parking lot, the restaurant was packed. The lunch hour tended to draw patrons from nearby businesses; at night, the place had more of a party atmosphere. The music would play, tables would be pushed aside to create a dance floor, and he was *definitely* looking forward to slow dancing with Kelsey.

He was looking forward to the entire evening with an anticipation that caught him off guard. After spilling his guts the way he had, escape should have been the only thing on his mind. He never talked about his past—*never*—and as little as two days ago, the thought of opening up about a time that still left him feeling lost and vulnerable would have tied his stomach into barbed-wire knots. And the thought of confiding in a Wilson!

Connor shook his head in disbelief, even as he admitted

Kelsey was no ordinary Wilson. She might not fit the Wilsons' model of perfection, but she fit his.

He rounded the car to open Kelsey's door, a split second too late, as it turned out. She already had one shapely leg extended, but he was in time to reach out a hand to help her out. Surprise lit her gaze, as if she hadn't considered his invitation to dinner a *real* date.

And despite the casual, last-minute offer, Connor realized he very much wanted this to be a real date. The kind of date where everyone in the restaurant would know Kelsey was with him. The kind where he never wanted the night to end and where, when the evening finally *did* end, a good-night kiss was not only expected, but breathlessly anticipated.

And when that time came, Connor vowed, he'd make sure there was no doubt in Kelsey's mind.

"You look amazing," he murmured, placing a hand at the small of her back.

Pleasure brightened her eyes and put color in her cheeks despite the less-than-original compliment. But hell, it was more than her looks. It was Kelsey. *She* amazed him.

"Thank you." She smoothed her hands over the embroidered skirt she wore. "I was hoping it wouldn't be too dressy."

"It's perfect." The flared skirt and off-the-shoulder blouse had a Spanish touch that emphasized her curves, and he wondered again how she could be so oblivious to how good she looked.

But that mix of confidence and insecurity was so much a part of Kelsey. He'd watched her divide the workload and make decisions without hesitation this afternoon, giving him an idea of how good a wedding coordinator she must be. Yet that confidence completely deserted her when it came to her personal life.

Living with the Wilsons had done that to her, Connor was

certain of it. They'd stripped her of her confidence, of her faith in her abilities, which they deemed worthless and beneath them.

Same way they'd declared *him* worthless and beneath them.

Connor shook off the dark thoughts as they stepped inside the restaurant. The scent of sizzling fajitas and salsa reminded him Trey hadn't been too far off about Sara's lunch. The caterer had brought delicate sandwiches and a fruit salad that looked more like a table centerpiece than something to eat.

"Man, I'm starving. I had a total slave driver nearly work me to death and only feed me bread and water."

"It was sandwiches, not just bread. And sparkling water, if that makes you feel any better." Kelsey laughed. "Besides, *you* volunteered, remember?"

"Yeah, I did." And he'd gladly do it again. Just looking into her excited brown eyes, listening to her laughter, made him feel—Connor thought for a moment, searching for the right word—happy. At peace. With nothing to prove, nothing to make up for. For the first time in his life, despite spilling the story of his sorry, less-than-sterling past, Connor felt he could be himself and that alone would be enough.

Except you didn't tell Kelsey the whole *story,* his conscience argued, dimming his contentment.

He hadn't told her about the money he'd taken, money he'd given to the Delgados to save the restaurant that pulsed with life around them. The business meant the world to Maria, especially following the dark days after her husband passed away. But Miguel's medical bills and the damage caused by an accidental grease fire had almost ruined the restaurant financially. In an effort to save it, Connor had taken the money from Gordon Wilson instead of throwing the check back in the smug SOB's face.

He knew what the older man thought. That he was nothing more than a gold-digging opportunist. But he was starting to think Kelsey might be the one Wilson, the one woman, to understand.

Was that why he'd invited her here? So she could meet Maria Delgado and see how important the woman was to him? So she could see for herself why he'd taken the money?

"Kelsey—"

"How about this? I'll pay for dinner tonight, compensation for all that slave labor?" she suggested as she stepped forward to talk to the hostess.

"Kelsey, wait." He caught her hand, wanting, *needing* to tell her the whole truth.

The seriousness in his tone made her eyes widen. "Hey, if you want to pay—"

"It's not that. I need to tell you—"

"Connor! *Mijo!*"

Hearing the familiar voice, Connor turned toward the sound with a large dose of relief and only the smallest amount of disappointment. The moment was gone, and he focused on Maria Delgado as she moved among the crowded tables toward him. She hadn't changed from the woman he remembered. Sure, she had a touch more gray in her waist-length hair and a few more wrinkles, but her dark eyes were as warm and welcoming as ever.

"Señora!" Connor bent to wrap his arms around the diminutive woman.

"My son told me you had come home! It is so good for you to be back!"

"It's good to see you, too." Seeing the undisguised interest in the older woman's eyes, he added, "Maria Delgado, this is Kelsey Wilson."

"Pleasure to meet you, Mrs. Delgado. Connor has told me a lot about you and how much your family means to him."

Maria beamed at him like a proud mother. "Connor, he is

family," she said to Kelsey. "And for him to bring you here, you must be very special. Never has he brought a young lady to the restaurant."

The implication that he'd brought Kelsey "home" to meet his family should have sent panic shooting like warning flares through his system, and yet seeing the two women talking and laughing together felt…*right.*

Kelsey also ignored the too-telling observation, but an adorable blush lit her cheeks as she added, "Your restaurant is amazing. I have to admit, I've never cared for Mexican food, but the quesadilla I had the other day was delicious."

"I always say, people who do not like Mexican food have not had *my* food." Maria pressed a hand against her bosom, pride shining in her dark eyes.

As Maria led them through a maze of crowded tables, Connor asked, "Where is Javy tonight?"

The *señora* waved a dismissive hand. "Ah, that boy. He is out with some girl. I tell him he needs to settle down, but does he listen? No. My son, he is too handsome for his own good. He does not have to work to get these girls' attention. Too often he chooses the easy way. He does not realize some things you must work for." She turned to Kelsey in a shared feminine confidence, a twinkle in her dark eyes. "But Connor, he is just handsome enough, no?"

"No. I mean, yes," Kelsey stuttered, flustered by the question. Connor was ready to jump in and rescue her from having to answer when she made her own save. "I think Connor is more than handsome enough," she said in a whisper plenty loud enough for him to overhear, "but he still has his work cut out for him."

Señora Delgado chortled and gave what sounded like a quick prayer beneath her breath. "Come, I will give you the best table in the house."

"I thought all the tables were the best tables," he teased with a wink at Kelsey as he placed his hand on the small of her back.

"Sí," the older woman agreed, "they are all the best."

Kelsey grinned, sharing his humor in the *señora's* unflappable logic.

After showing them to a secluded table in the back, Maria kissed Connor's cheek and went back to work. Kelsey's hand touched the ladder-back chair, but Connor beat her to it. As he pulled it out for her, he leaned close. Close enough to catch the cinnamon scent of her skin. Close enough to see the freckles she'd tried to hide beneath makeup. Close enough to hear her breath catch in reaction to his nearness. "You should know by now, Kelsey," he murmured, "I'm not afraid of a little hard work."

Her eyes widened, but just like she had with Señora Delgado, Kelsey found her own footing and knocked him for a loop when she said, "I'm counting on it."

Time froze as the moment held them in its grip. The restaurant, with its loud music and bright lights, faded away, leaving behind only Kelsey's gorgeous brown eyes and softly parted lips. A burst of laughter from a nearby table broke the moment, and Kelsey sank into the chair he held for her. Connor had little choice but to take his own seat and curse the table separating them.

A waiter came by with menus, but Connor could tell by the frequent glances she sent his way Kelsey's mind wasn't on dinner. Finally she set the menu aside and said, "Is it true what Señora Delgado said before? You never brought anyone here?"

He'd let her get away with the unasked question before, but not this time. "Come on, Kelsey. Are you interested in *anybody* or in Emily?"

At first she looked ready to protest, only to square her

shoulders and meet his gaze head-on. "Okay. Did you ever bring Emily here?"

"No. The Delgados are like family to me, and I wasn't sure Emily would get that." He hadn't been able to picture Emily at the rustic, homey restaurant. He still couldn't…and yet Kelsey fit in so perfectly. He'd never had a doubt about bringing *her.*

Not waiting for her to ask why—or wanting to look too closely for a reason himself—Connor pushed back from the table. Kelsey's eyes widened in surprise as he held out his hand and said, "Come on. Let's dance."

As Kelsey took Connor's hand, it occurred to her that she had no idea how to dance to the Latin-flavored beat pulsing from the speakers. But that didn't stop her from following him onto the tiny dance floor, where the music instantly switched to a ballad.

Connor's smile flashed as he pulled her into his arms. "Couldn't have planned it better myself."

"I'm not so sure you didn't."

"This wasn't me. It must be fate."

Kelsey didn't know about fate, but being held in Connor's arms certainly felt like a dream. She wasn't the only one who had dressed up for the evening. Connor had showered and shaved, brushed his dark hair back from his forehead. A touch of sexy sophistication replaced a bit of his bad-boy image thanks to the white button-down shirt and black slacks he wore instead of his usual T-shirt and jeans. No matter what Maria Delgado said about her son, it was Connor who took Kelsey's breath away. He was the most gorgeous man she'd ever met, and the sheer look of masculine appreciation in his eyes made her feel beautiful. But even as the physical connection robbed her of her breath, the emotional connection threatened to steal her heart.

Listening to him talk about his past and seeing his love for Señora Delgado revealed a different side of Connor. A fiercely loyal and caring side that would be as easy to fall for as his cocky grin and killer body.

Right, her conscience told her. *And the fact that Connor never shared that side of himself with Emily, never told her about his childhood, never brought her to the restaurant, that has* nothing *to do with it.*

Kelsey wanted to shove the goading voice aside, but it was impossible to ignore. Connor had trusted her with the heartbreak of his past and a happier part of his present, and it was almost impossible not to think of the future. Not a forever future, of course, but the immediate future—and how she'd gladly spend what time she and Connor had left in his arms.

For the first time in years, Kelsey didn't feel like she'd come in a distant second to her too-beautiful cousin, an irony her disapproving conscience couldn't overlook, as Connor was the one man in a position to best make comparisons…

"You're too quiet," Connor murmured in her ear. "It makes me nervous."

Kelsey laughed at the thought of *anything* making Connor nervous. "Don't be. I was just thinking."

"Hmm. Those might be the most nerve-racking words a man ever hears. Should I ask *what* you've been thinking?"

Not brave enough to admit the whole truth, Kelsey said, "Only that we don't have much time left."

Connor cocked an eyebrow. "Until the wedding?"

"Until you leave."

"Ready to see me go, huh?"

"Surprisingly, no," Kelsey said, although Connor didn't seem surprised by her admission.

Because it was so obvious how her heart slammed into her chest every time he came near? How her knees turned to jelly with a single look? It wasn't something she wanted to admit to herself, forget giving Connor that kind of ammunition. Because even though telling her about his past and bringing her to meet his surrogate mother might have melted the walls around her heart, nothing said Connor felt the same.

"Good," he said. "Since I'm not ready to leave."

"Because you haven't figured Todd out yet?"

Connor scoffed. "I did that a long time ago. No, it's you I'm still trying to figure out."

This time it was Kelsey's turn to laugh. "I'm no mystery. I've already spilled all my secrets."

"I think there's more to discover. But I've already figured out a few things on my own. Like how you feel in my arms…how you taste when I kiss you…how I can make you blush without even trying."

Feeling her face heat, Kelsey protested, "Like you aren't trying right now."

"Naw," he said with a grin that did more than make her face heat as he lifted a hand and traced a pattern on her cheek. "If I was really trying to make you blush, I'd tell you how much this star on your cheek turns me on—especially when I think about all the other shapes I might find…and where I might find them."

Kelsey swallowed. She'd spent her whole life hating the freckles that marked her pale skin, but in a split second, in a single sentence, Connor had made her forget every teasing comment, every self-conscious thought.

"Connor." The lone word was all she could manage, but every bit of the emotion she felt echoed in her voice.

Making a sound deep in his throat that could have been a groan, he protested, "Don't look at me like that or I'll end up doing something not meant to be done in public."

Kelsey did lower her gaze, from the hunger in his eyes and

past his too-tempting lips, to stare at his throat. Not because of what he'd said, but because she didn't have the courage to look him in the face and say what she wanted to say. "There are…more private places."

Connor's arms flexed, pulling her closer, and his voice was a deep rumble in her ear as he said, "My hotel room."

Seemingly without conscious thought, an image flashed in Kelsey's mind—Emily leaving Connor's room—and she blurted out, "My house."

Bringing their dance to a halt, Connor stepped back slightly and nudged her chin up. "Are you sure?"

Even though he was asking about so much more than a simple destination, Kelsey met his gaze and repeated, "My house."

She felt slightly guilty as Connor pulled her through the restaurant. "Shouldn't we say goodbye?"

"Maria'll understand," Connor insisted without breaking stride.

Deciding she'd rather not think about how much the woman might understand, Kelsey focused on keeping up with Connor's long strides. Her heart pounded wildly in her chest, but the crazed rhythm had less to do with how fast they were going and so much more to do with what would happen once they got back to her place. And Kelsey didn't think Connor could walk fast enough….

And he must have felt the same, she realized when they reached the car. Instead of unlocking the door, Connor turned and pulled her into his arms.

"I've wanted to do this from the moment I saw you."

The husky words would have been easier to believe had Kelsey spoken them, but coming from Connor, they sent a thrill rushing through her as enticing as his kiss. "You wanted to do this at the airport?"

"At the airport. In your car on the way from the airport. The first time we came to the restaurant." His voice dropped to a husky murmur. "My hotel room."

Kelsey shivered, her thoughts instantly turning to the king-size bed where she wouldn't have to imagine the press of Connor's body against her own. His green eyes glowed as if he'd read her thoughts and was right there…in his hotel bed…with her.

Ducking his head, he caught her lips in a kiss that picked up right where the last had left off. The hunger and intensity didn't have to build; passion and desire had shimmered between them all evening like desert heat. Kelsey sank her hands into his dark hair, her fingers sifting through the silky strands. With Connor leaning against the side of the car, Kelsey didn't have to stretch to reach his mouth; they were perfectly aligned—lips to lips, chest to chest, thigh to thigh.

Connor slid his hands down her back, his fingers claiming the soft flesh of her hips as he pulled her tighter into the vee of his body. Kelsey thought if it were possible to pass out from pure pleasure, she might sink to the ground on the spot.

Instead, she broke away from his kiss. Hiding her face against his neck, she murmured, "My house, remember?" And then she gave in to temptation and pressed her mouth to the strong column of his throat, right where his pulse pounded in time with the pulsing Latin beat coming from the restaurant.

His throat jerked as he swallowed, and he pushed away from the car door without breaking their embrace. He reached back for the door handle and fumbled for a second before he broke away with a muffled curse and twisted around to get a better grip. But instead of pulling the door open, Connor paused, hand in the air as if he'd forgotten what he was doing. Seeming to shake off the hesitation, he opened the door for her.

But in that split-second hesitation, the intensity dissipated like smoke from a doused fire. Her heart still pounded from the kiss, and her breath was far from steady, but the mood had definitely changed. He wouldn't meet her gaze, and Kelsey couldn't help wondering… "Connor, what's wrong? Did I do something—"

"No," he bit out. His fierce expression lessened when he saw her flinch, but frustration filled his movements as he ran a hand through his hair. "No, you didn't do anything wrong. It's just—this is crazy. *You* make me crazy! I haven't made out with a girl in a car since Emily, and now here I am with another Wilson—"

His words cut off abruptly, but not before the small thrill Kelsey experienced at the thought of driving Connor McClane crazy was buried by a wave of doubt and insecurity as she imagined Connor and Emily making out in a car.

And—could this really *get* any worse—not just any car. The vintage Mustang belonged to Javy, who'd undoubtedly owned it for years. Back when Connor would have borrowed the hot car to pick up Emily…

Humiliation burning in her cheeks, Kelsey wanted nothing more than to go home, but she dreaded getting in that car. It didn't matter that she and Connor had already driven all over town in it; now, all she could see was Emily in the passenger seat, wind whipping through her blond hair. Emily, searching for a favorite song on the radio. Emily, slipping into the back seat where Connor waited…

"This was a mistake."

"Kelsey—"

"Can we go?" she interrupted. Maybe if she closed her eyes, she could picture herself somewhere else.

"No."

"What?"

Connor's dark frown told her she'd definitely heard right the first time. "No. I'm not gonna let you run off."

"There's nothing else to talk about, Connor. You and Emily—"

"All right. Fine. Let's talk about how there hasn't been a 'me and Emily' for *years.* I can't change my past, and I can't change yours."

"*My* past?"

"How much of this is about me and Emily? And how much of it is about *you* and Emily? How many times have you felt you couldn't live up to your cousins? How many times have the Wilsons made you feel second best?"

How many? Kelsey couldn't count the numerous times she'd tried walking in her cousins' footsteps only to fall in disgrace again and again. "Uncle Gordon and Aunt Charlene treated me *exactly* like they treated Aileen and Emily. But that was the problem. I'm—not like those girls."

"You don't have to be, Kelsey. You're you. That's more than enough."

Honesty and desire glowed in Connor's eyes. But as much as she longed to believe him, as she slid into the passenger seat Kelsey couldn't help feeling like she was trying yet again to fill Emily's place.

Shoving the key into the ignition, Connor started the car, and they were silent throughout the ride back to Kelsey's; the rumble of the engine was the only sound. Only as they pulled into her driveway did she find the courage to ask the question shouting through her thoughts the whole time.

"Why did you stop? If it wasn't about Emily—"

Connor sighed. "We were in the middle of a public parking lot where anyone could walk by. I should have the self-control to keep my hands to myself. But being back here has me acting like a hotheaded kid again. *You* make me feel like a hotheaded kid," he practically growled, not sounding the least bit happy about the idea. "Not Emily. *You.*"

"I want to believe you. But this is all happening so fast, and it isn't easy to change how I feel after a matter of days!"

"I know. But I'm gonna keep trying."

Connor walked her to the front door, where he leaned close, giving her ample time to pull away. If his earlier kiss had struck like a flash of lightning, this was like the slow promise of a sunrise. Kelsey felt the gentle rays first, the touch of warmth against her cheeks as his fingers slid into her hair. And then light blazed behind her eyelids as he kissed her.

Heat poured through her, starting where his mouth brushed against hers then spreading out to all parts of her body, all the way down to her tingling fingertips and toes. Just when he'd left her knees weak and her willpower completely shaken, he eased away, ending the kiss slowly, reluctantly. "I want to see you tomorrow."

"I can't—"

"Kelsey."

"Not because of, well, anything. I'm busy tomorrow."

"With your shop?"

Kelsey shook her head regretfully. "The shop will have to wait a few days. I'm meeting Emily for brunch, and then we're going shopping for bridesmaids' gifts. Assuming that doesn't take all day, I have to meet with a friend who's putting together an audiovisual presentation for the reception."

"What time?"

"In the afternoon."

"Dunworthy has a meeting set up for tomorrow at six. Interested in another stakeout?"

Kelsey forced herself not to look over at the Mustang. The vehicle had somehow turned into so much more than a simple car. It was a physical reminder of Connor's past with Emily. A past Kelsey wasn't sure she could ignore. "Do I even want to know how you came across the information?"

"Nothing illegal. I got it the old-fashioned way. I overheard a conversation he was having on his cell phone." Connor frowned. "Well, I guess the cell phone part isn't old-fashioned, but the eavesdropping was."

"It could be nothing. A dead end like the other day."

"Could be. Wanna find out?" His eyebrows rose in exaggerated challenge, and Kelsey couldn't say no.

"See you tomorrow."

Kelsey knew she should open the door and step inside instead of gazing after Connor like a lovesick teenager, but she couldn't tear her gaze away as he walked down her driveway to the car.

He turned back before she had the chance to duck indoors, seeming unsurprised to find her staring after him. "There's something you should know, Kelsey. I might have kissed your cousin in this car. But I never slept with her."

"In the car?"

His lips kicked up in a smile, but the look in his eyes was completely serious. "Or anywhere else."

Chapter Eight

The next afternoon, standing in her sun-filled kitchen, Kelsey poured steaming black coffee into a thermal mug. She'd tossed and turned most of the night, her sleep plagued by dreams. Even now, she was haunted by images of gliding down an endless, rose-strewn runner toward her groom—toward Connor—only to watch, helpless, as he smiled his devastating smile and walked away with Emily.

"It's just a stupid dream," she muttered, as if speaking the words aloud might give them more strength. "I'm not marrying Connor. I'm not *falling* for Connor."

So she'd had temporary a lapse of judgment, of sanity. She'd been caught in the moment—the restaurant's party atmosphere, the sexy rhythm of the music that had seeped into her soul and pulsed in her veins…

Oh, who are you kidding? an all-too-knowing voice

demanded. She hadn't been caught up in the moment; she'd been caught up in the man.

Maybe she should ask Emily how she'd dated Connor for months *without* sleeping with him. Although Emily never divulged intimate details, Kelsey assumed they had made love. Now that she'd met Connor, it seemed even harder to believe Emily—or any woman—could resist.

Knowing now that Emily *had* resisted made Kelsey wonder if her cousin's feelings for Connor were as strong as she'd once believed, or if Connor was right and Emily had only been using him. What was it he'd said—he was Emily's lone act of rebellion? But even if that were true, it didn't necessarily change his feelings. Maybe coming back wasn't about picking up where they'd left off, but about finally taking that relationship further.

Her stomach felt more than a little sick at the thought, and she thrust the glass pot back into the machine, grabbed the to-go lid and slapped it onto the mug. But her aim must have been slightly off, and the cup tipped, splashing coffee over the countertop.

Gasping, Kelsey dove for a manila envelope lying nearby, snatching it out of the way of the java flood. She clutched the package to her chest with a relieved sigh. Emily's life in pictures filled the envelope, most dating back to the days prior to digital CDs.

Kelsey shuddered at the thought of telling her aunt she'd ruined the photos of Emily's first piano recital, first ballet, first play. She had to get back in control. Her near destruction of the photographs was a small symptom of a larger problem.

She was letting Connor get under her skin.

She'd taken possession of her own shop the day before, the realization of a dream that sometimes seemed as old as she was. Her thoughts should have been consumed by plans for polishing the place until it shined, expanding her nonexistent advertising budget, hiring the support staff Lisa had mentioned.

Instead Connor filled her thoughts and her dreams, and was far too close to edging his way into her heart. Was this how her mother felt when she met her father? Kelsey wondered. Had Donnie Mardell become more important to Olivia than her own hopes and dreams? More important than her own family?

Kelsey forced herself not to panic. Surely she wouldn't make that big a mistake, not with her mother's life as an example. How many times had Olivia warned Kelsey to rely on herself and not to risk leaning on someone who would let her down in the end?

"Wilson women against the world," Kelsey murmured, the familiar motto calming her as she set the envelope safely aside and unrolled a swath of paper towels.

The sudden sound of the doorbell caught her off guard. She didn't have time for unexpected guests any more than she had time for unexpected doubts. Dropping the paper towels over the spilled coffee, she headed toward the front door as the bell pealed again. After a quick glance through the peephole, Kelsey pulled the door open.

As if her thoughts had somehow conjured him out of thin air, Connor leaned against the doorway. How was it that he looked better every time she saw him? Was it because she now knew his shoulders were as strong as they looked? How solid his chest had felt beneath her hands? How his hair had felt like warm silk against her fingers? And how his mouth had worked magic against her own?

"Hey, Kelsey," he said before striding inside.

Trailing after him as if *he* owned the place and she was the uninvited guest, she asked, "What are you doing here?"

He stopped to face her, a frown replacing his cocky smile. "I thought you were coming with me. Todd's meeting, remember?"

"That's not until six," she protested as she walked into the kitchen to the mess she'd left behind.

"What happened in here?"

As much as she would have liked to lay the blame at Connor's feet, she said, "Don't ask." She balled up the soggy paper towels, groaning at the coffee-colored stain left behind on her beige Formica, and tossed them into the trash. She grabbed the envelope of photographs and her purse and brushed by Connor on the way to the door.

"I have to meet my friend about the audio-video presentation for the reception, remember?"

Connor shrugged. "So we go there first and stake out the meeting after."

She should say no. She should keep him far, far away, and not just because of the havoc he might wreak on Emily's wedding. "I'm already running late." As a flat-out denial, the words fell short.

"So let's go."

"Okay, but—" Kelsey straightened her shoulders. "I'll drive." She should have known it wouldn't make any difference how matter-of-factly she made that statement, Connor would see through it.

Judging by the look in his dark eyes, he did see—straight through to her heart. "Sounds like I need to work even harder."

"Connor—"

"It's okay," he interrupted. He stepped closer, and Kelsey tensed, half in preparation to defend her decision and half in anticipation of his approach. But nothing could have readied her for Connor cupping the back of her neck and pulling her into a kiss.

To her dismay, it ended before it even began. A quick press of lips again her own, and then it was over. And Kelsey had to clench her hands into fists to keep from grabbing the front of Connor's T-shirt and demand that he do it again. That he do it *right.*

As he pulled away, he gazed at her flustered—heated—face and smiled. "I never could resist a challenge."

"Are you sure this is right?" Kelsey asked.

Connor's directions to Todd's meeting had brought them to a Scottsdale neighborhood that rivaled her aunt and uncle's when it came to exclusivity, opulence and sheer expense. The winding roads led them past multileveled mansions surrounded by artfully arranged desert landscapes, sparkling water fountains and wrought-iron gates.

They were practically the first words she'd spoken since they'd dropped off Emily's pictures earlier. Kelsey had been grateful to focus on the straightforward directions of right, left, north and south rather than try to traverse the dangerous path her heart was traveling down.

Catching a street sign carved into a boulder, Connor said, "Turn here. This is it."

"Nice place." Irony filled Kelsey's voice at the understated description. The two-story home had a circular entryway, decorative columns, and floor-to-ceiling windows.

When she tapped on the brake, Connor insisted, "Don't stop." With a glance out the back, he said, "Okay. We should be good here. Go ahead and turn around."

Kelsey glanced in the rearview mirror. Thanks to a neighboring oleander hedge, she could barely see the house. Hopefully Todd wouldn't notice the two of them lurking in her car a block away. After turning the car to face the house, she asked, "Now what?"

"Now we wait."

Kelsey sighed. "I don't think I have the patience for being a private eye."

Connor's lips quirked into a smile. "That's okay. I'm not planning on changing careers and becoming a wedding coordinator, either. Besides, it's almost six."

"Todd will be late," Kelsey predicted. "He's always late." Tardiness was one of her aunt's pet peeves. A sign, according to Charlene Wilson, that showed a person believed his time more important than those around him. Somehow, though, she smothered her annoyance when it came to Todd.

"So he isn't perfect after all."

"I never said he was."

Connor made a thoughtful sound but hardly embraced her words. No surprise. *She* wasn't the one Connor wanted to impress. He was determined to prove her aunt and uncle wrong about Todd. But would that really be enough to make Connor let go of the past? Would Connor ever believe he was good enough, or would it take being good enough for Emily for him to see his own worth?

She sighed and sank lower in the seat, not wanting to think too hard on the answer to that question. Seconds later a car rounded the corner, and Kelsey impulsively grabbed Connor's arm. "Look!"

Her heart skipped a beat at the feel of his warm skin and muscle beneath her palm. When he leaned closer for a better look, her pulse quickened.

A woman sat behind the wheel of the luxury car, and Kelsey wondered if Connor might get his proof. Neither of them spoke as they waited for Todd's arrival and the meeting to unfold. Ten minutes later, Todd's SUV pulled up. When he climbed from the vehicle and casually glanced in their direction, Kelsey gasped.

"Relax," Connor advised. "He can't see us."

As she focused on the scene outside, Kelsey frowned in confusion. Todd flashed a smile at the woman as he walked up the driveway, but when he reached out to shake the woman's hand, the gesture was not only platonic but professional.

Connor swore. "I don't believe it. That woman's a Realtor. There's a lockbox on the front door."

Sure enough, the brunette led Todd to the front door, where she opened the small box and pulled out a key. With a flourish she turned the handle and waved Todd inside. Since Emily hadn't mentioned a new home, Kelsey wondered if the place was a wedding gift. Despite her questionable opinion of the man, she couldn't help feeling impressed by the romantic and extravagant gesture.

"We should go."

"Just—wait," Connor ground out.

A few minutes later Todd and the Realtor exited the house. Judging by the smile on the woman's face, Kelsey assumed the meeting had gone well. She shook Todd's hand again, nodded enthusiastically over whatever he said, and waved as he drove off.

"That's that," Kelsey said as she reached for the ignition. Connor stopped her with a touch, closing his hand over hers and slipping the keys out of her grasp before she ever realized his intention. "Connor, what—"

"Come on."

Connor kept a firm grip on Kelsey's hand as they walked toward the house despite her repeated tugs and her sharply whispered protests. As long as he had the keys, she couldn't go anywhere without him. So why exactly was she trying to pull away? The better question: why was he still hanging on?

"Connor! Stop! We're going to get caught!"

"Doing what? You know, I'm really starting to wonder about this guilty conscience of yours."

"You should," she muttered, "considering I didn't *have* one until you came along."

The front door opened, and Kelsey dug in her heels deep enough to leave divots in the grass. The Realtor looked surprised, but only for a moment. Professional smile in place, she asked, "Are you two interested in the property?"

Kelsey's grip tightened on Connor's hand. A quick glance in her direction revealed a panicked look that screamed *busted.* Fortunately, he had a bit more experience when it came to covering his butt, as well as any curvaceous female backside he dragged along for the ride.

Flashing a smile, he said, "My fiancée and I were driving through the neighborhood and noticed the lockbox. We don't have an appointment, but—"

"Oh, I'd love to show you around."

The inside of the house lived up to the exterior's elegant promise. Gorgeous views, a wide-open floor plan and every upgrade imaginable—travertine floors, granite countertops, stainless-steel appliances. The decor matched the surrounding desert with golds and browns and a hint of green.

"The house is beautiful," Kelsey said, once she'd realized the Realtor wasn't going to accuse them of trespassing.

"It's only been on the market a few days," the Realtor said as she concluded the six-bedroom, four-bath, media-room tour back at the front entry. "Another couple is interested in the property for their first place."

"Right. 'Cause this is the perfect starter home," Connor muttered.

Kelsey opened her mouth, ready to insist she didn't need a mansion, only to remember she and Connor weren't engaged. They wouldn't need a starter home or any other kind.

"Out of curiosity," he said, "can you tell how much the other couple is offering?"

The woman's smile was both sympathetic and hopeful. "I don't think money was an issue, but I have several other properties I'd be more than willing to show you." She pulled a card from her pocket and held it out to Connor. "Give me a call, and I can give you a list of houses that might fit your lifestyle."

Connor managed a nod, but as they walked out of the house, he crushed her card in his hand. *"Fit my lifestyle,"* he bit out. "Not to mention my budget."

His body thrummed with frustration, and Kelsey expected him to chuck the card into the street. Finally he shoved it into his pocket and stalked toward her car.

Kelsey didn't bother to ask for her keys back when Connor automatically went to the driver's-side door. Instead, she slid into the passenger seat. Trying for a practical tone, she said, "We already knew Todd has money."

"Yeah, we did," he said with a grim twist to his lips. "I'm starting to think the guy might be perfect after all."

"No one's perfect," Kelsey insisted. "Everyone has their faults and—"

"And the Wilsons certainly saw mine."

"You were a kid," she argued. "You can't believe what happened back then has anything to do with the man you are now."

Muttering what sounded suspiciously like "Don't be so sure," he cranked the engine and peeled away from the house.

Kelsey slapped a hand down on the armrest, but her tight grip slowly loosened. Despite his obvious frustration, Connor kept the car under perfect control. Within minutes they were on the freeway, but the turn he took wouldn't lead to her house.

Streetlights flickered on as daylight faded, marking the way toward an older part of Phoenix. They passed an abandoned drive-in, a boarded-up gas station and liquor store, the only business likely to thrive in such a depressing neighborhood. She could have asked where they were going, but as they drove by houses with peeling paint and duct-taped windows, lawns choked by weeds and neglect, she already knew.

A few minutes later Connor braked to a halt, gravel crunching beneath the wheels. He didn't say anything or make a move to get out of the car. With both hands still gripping the wheel, he stared at the trailer park across the street.

Kelsey had seen plenty of mobile home communities before. Manufactured homes, they were called now. Houses laid out in neat rows, with flower beds and swimming pools like any other nice, little neighborhood.

This was not that kind of place. The dirt lot, with its haphazard trailers and junkyard of vehicles, made the use of the term *park* an irony. The murmur of the engine was the only sound until Connor gave a sudden, harsh bark of laughter. "This is it. Where I came from. Who I am."

"No, it isn't." Unlocking her seat belt, Kelsey shifted on the seat to face him. The fading sunset glowed in the distance, casting his profile in bronze. "This isn't you any more than where I grew up makes me who I am."

"You're a Wilson. You're—"

Connor cut himself off, giving Kelsey the chance to interject, "I *am* a Wilson. But I'm not Emily. I'm not Aileen. And I wasn't raised like them."

"I know. On the outside looking in," he said, as he turned to look at her. Face-to-face, Kelsey could see the gold flecks in his green eyes. "That's what I thought when I first met you. The Wilson outsider."

That insight, pointing how she'd always felt—a part of and yet apart from her family—made Kelsey feel as if Connor knew her better than anyone. His words and the tenderness in his gaze crept inside her chest and wrapped around her heart. Somehow, being on the outside didn't matter so much when he was there with her. "You were right," she said softly.

But if he could somehow see inside her, Kelsey felt she was starting to do the same and getting to know the real Connor. His coming back to Arizona had to do with more than simply disliking Todd or even with proving her family wrong. His return had to do with a guilt *inside* him. As if by stopping the wedding, he could somehow make up for a past he could not change.

"And maybe that's why I can see you so clearly. This isn't who you are, Connor," she repeated. "Maybe it's who you were, but that's all. I've seen who you are now. You're a good friend, a good man—"

A sound rose in Connor's throat, part denial, part despair, and he jerked open the car door as if desperate for escape. Kelsey winced as he slammed it behind him, but she didn't hesitate to follow. He couldn't shut her out that easily!

"Connor, wait!" She scrambled out of the car after him, trying to keep up with the long strides that carried him across the weed-and-trash-strewn lot. She gasped as her foot hit an uneven spot on the heaved asphalt. She took a tottering step, arms windmilling for balance, but gravity won the battle, and she hit the ground.

"Kelsey!" Connor swore beneath his breath. "Are you okay?"

With a close-up view of the weeds and trash littering the trailer lot, Kelsey felt a moment's relief that she hadn't landed in a black, greasy puddle inches from her face.

"I'm fine," she insisted, even as Connor leaned down to help her up. Flames of heat licked at her. Some from the heel of her hand that had scraped across the pavement, some from the blazing heat bouncing off the black surface, but mostly from the sheer embarrassment of Connor witnessing her utter clumsiness. "Really, I—" She sucked in a quick breath as he took her hand to pull her to her feet.

Beneath his tanned skin, Connor went pale. "You're hurt."

Taking a hesitant glance down, she breathed out a sigh of

relief. "It's nothing. Only a scratch." A few thin lines of blood showed through the abraded skin on her palm, but other than the slight sting, she was fine.

Running his thumb gently across the scrape as if he could heal by touch alone, Connor said, "I never should have brought you here. It's my fault."

"It was an accident that could have happened in front of my own shop! It is *not* your fault." Gentling her voice, she added, "You're not responsible for every bad thing that happens. I don't know why you feel that way, but Connor, looking for dirt on Todd won't change things. Especially when—" she took a deep breath, reluctant to say the words but knowing she had to "—when it doesn't seem like there's anything to find."

"There is," he said flatly, refusing to consider failure. "Jake's still following a lead in St. Louis, and I'm not giving up here. I know guys like Dunworthy. He can only keep up this golden boy B.S. for so long. He's gonna slip. The closer it gets to the wedding, the more pressure there's gonna be, and he'll slip. I know it—"

"In your gut," Kelsey finished with a sigh. She turned her hand within his. Even through that light touch, she could feel the tension tightening his shoulders and arms and radiating down to the fingers she linked with hers. As gently as she could, she suggested, "Maybe it's time to stop listening to your gut."

"I can't." He gritted the words out of clenched teeth.

"Why not?"

"Because the last time I didn't listen, a woman was nearly killed."

Connor reached over and cranked the car's air conditioner to full blast, even though he doubted the frigid air would help. Sweat soaked the back of his neck, but it had little to do with the outside temperature despite the hundred-plus heat. The relentless sun, which bounced off every shiny surface to pinpoint on him as if he were a bug trapped beneath a kid's magnifying glass, had nothing on Kelsey's questioning glances.

He felt as if he was burning up from the inside out…all thanks to four little words.

You're a good man.

Kelsey had looked him straight in the eye with those words, her soft voice packing the same punch as a sonic boom. He didn't deserve that kind of faith. He'd disappointed too many women in the past: his mother, Emily, Cara Mitchell…

The more Kelsey trusted in him, the more he longed to believe in that trust, the worse it would be when he finally, irrevocably, let her down.

He sucked in a lungful of air, the heat threatening to suffocate him. He needed space—space to breathe, space to run, space that wasn't filled with Kelsey's cinnamon scent, her concerned glances, her soft voice…

"Connor…"

She was going to ask him what happened with Cara. His grip tightened on the passenger armrest, inches from the door handle and escape…even if escape meant paying the price for hitting the ground running at forty miles an hour.

No, telling truth was better. More painful, maybe, but at least Kelsey would realize he wasn't the man she thought he was.

"One of the first things I learned after opening my business was that you don't turn down work. You might not like the job, you might not like the client, but if it pays the bills, you take the job."

Kelsey slowed for a red light. Freedom beckoned, but Connor kept his hand on the armrest. "I didn't like Doug Mitchell. I didn't like the job, even though catching cheating spouses has always been part of the P.I. business. My gut told me he was bad news, but I didn't listen."

Silence filled the car, and Kelsey's gaze was as tangible as the trickle of sweat running from his temple. "What happened?" she murmured.

"I did what I was paid to do. I followed Cara Mitchell. To the grocery store, the salon, the gym… It was tedious, boring," he added, reminded of the conversation they'd had waiting for Dunworthy's meeting. "And I thought maybe Doug was wrong. That he was worried about nothing and his marriage was one of the few that would make it."

His hand cramped, and try as he might, he couldn't loosen his grip. His fingers seemed to have melded into the padded vinyl. "But then, one Tuesday, Cara drove south on the freeway. And I kept thinking it was Tuesday, and Tuesday was art class. So why was she going in the wrong direction? Before long, she ended up at a motel and when this guy opened the door, I thought here we go. I was wrong, and Doug was right."

"So she was having an affair?"

"Sure seemed that way," he said with a grimace. "Meeting some guy, staying behind closed shades, and leaving an hour later with her hair mussed and her makeup smudged… What else would you think?"

"What did *you* think?"

"I—I didn't know. It was suspicious, sure. But it wasn't proof, you know? Not one hundred percent take-it-to-the-bank proof. And in my gut I didn't believe it. Maybe I'd gotten too close. It happens, P.I.s falling for their marks, but that wasn't it. I wasn't attracted to Cara Mitchell. But I guess I—*liked* her. Respected her. She smiled at kids in the store, took the time to talk to little old ladies. She told cashiers when they gave her back too much change! I just didn't believe she was having an affair. But her husband wanted an update. He was the client, and he paid to know what I'd seen."

"But…you didn't actually *see* anything."

Connor winced at her logical protest. "And that's exactly what I told Doug. Only it didn't matter. Far as he was concerned, I'd seen enough and was off the job."

If only it had ended there…

"I couldn't get over my gut feeling that I was wrong. Wrong about Cara, wrong about what I'd seen. I thought if I followed her a few more days, I'd know for sure." Kelsey hit the gas as another red light turned green, and Connor desperately wished he was still the one driving. He'd go from zero to sixty in a split second if pure speed would give him the chance to outrun his memories.

"I was across the street watching when Doug came home from work in the middle of the day. I don't know if he hoped to catch Cara in the act, or if his rage and jealousy got to be too much. I heard her scream. I rushed into the house."

"But you stopped Doug, right?"

"Not soon enough. Cara was badly beaten and nearly unconscious by the time I got into the house and pulled Doug off her."

He could still see her, bloody and bruised, lying on the floor because of him. "The guy she went to see was a counselor. He'd rented the motel room to give her a safe place to stay, but he couldn't convince her to leave Doug, even though he'd been abusing her for years. If I'd listened to my gut—"

"But you *did* listen. You listened when you knew you didn't have the whole story. Cara Mitchell would likely be dead if not for you. You saved her life, Connor."

"If I hadn't taken the job—"

"Someone else would have. Someone who wouldn't have *cared* about a gut feeling. Once the job was over, that would have been it. They wouldn't have given Cara Mitchell a second thought."

Connor opened his mouth, ready to argue, but Kelsey's words ran deeper into his soul, soothing some of his guilt. Not that he believed he was any kind of hero. But he'd witnessed Doug's determination. He wasn't the type of guy to give up easily. Had Connor turned down the job, Doug *would* have found another P.I.

"Maybe—maybe you're right."

As Kelsey stopped for another red light, she turned to meet his gaze straight on. "I know I am," she said with the same certainty as when she'd vowed he was a good man.

Would she still think so when he told her about the money her uncle had paid him to leave town? No one had ever put the kind of faith and trust in him that Kelsey did, and every ounce of self-preservation inside him resisted the thought of telling her the truth.

Even if she gave him the chance to explain, even if she understood his reasons, the truth would change things. And yet he had to tell her. If he wanted her to believe he truly was a good man, if *he* wanted to believe that, he had to tell her.

But not tonight. There'd already been enough revelations about the past. And in case finding out about the money did change things, well, Connor selfishly wanted to hold on to Kelsey's faith in him for a little while longer.

"You know, this isn't necessary." Side by side on her couch, Kelsey watched as Connor placed the last piece of tape over the bandage on her hand. As far as a protest went, her words were pretty weak. Just like the rest of her, she thought.

Connor smoothed his thumb across her palm, his gaze intent on his task. A lock of dark hair had fallen across his forehead, shadowing his eyes and adding the slightest touch of softness to the hard planes and angles of his features.

Little shocks zapped up her arm, but it had nothing to do with pain. If she hadn't been sitting next to Connor, she probably would have melted into a puddle at his feet.

"It would have been tricky to do this on your own. Besides, it was the least I could do," he said, guilt and concern filling his expression as his hand rose to brush her hair back from her cheek.

And Kelsey couldn't resist his caring side any more than she'd been able to resist the other facets of his personality: the bad boy, the loyal friend, the protective warrior. They all combined to make up the man Connor was—the man Kelsey loved.

Her every instinct shouted in denial, but it was a useless protest. She'd been falling for him since the moment they met, a slow-motion tumble that landed her in this place, in this time, in his arms…

The intimacy of the moment pulled her closer. Her job, her family, even Connor's relationship with Emily seemed like distant, insignificant concerns. His fingers tunneled into her hair. Her amazing hair, Kelsey thought, recalling the words he'd spoken outside of Todd's office. She hadn't believed him then, but she did now. On the day she confronted him in his hotel room, he'd demanded she prove her loyalty to Emily, and she'd told him actions, not words, proved how a person truly felt. And Connor was a man of action, and he proved his feelings by trusting *her*—with his past, with his close friendship with the Delgados. How could she do anything but trust him in return?

"The last thing I'd ever want to do is hurt you, Kelsey," he vowed, that sense of responsibility carving a groove between his eyebrows.

"You didn't," she promised. "You won't."

Despite her words, doubt lingered in his gaze. Leaning forward, she brushed her lips against his, actions once again backing up words. Because whether Connor knew it or not, she *was* his. Body and soul. She shifted closer but couldn't get close enough.

Her hands charted a course her body longed to make, following a path from his shoulders to his chest, where she could feel his heart pounding a wild rhythm, and to his flat stomach and muscled thighs, which tensed beneath her hands.

Connor's hands stayed buried in her hair, but like the emotional connection moments before, the physical connection was so deep that with her every touch her own body responded. She felt the brush of his fingers trailing from her collarbones down to her breasts, to her stomach, ticklish enough to tremble at the imaginary contact.

Connor ended the kiss for a much needed breath but kept his mouth pressed to her cheek, her jaw, her throat…

A shrill buzz started them both. After the first few bars, Connor recognized his phone's ring tone, but the electronic device—one he never went anywhere without—was the last thing on his mind. He nearly groaned in frustration at the very thought of ending the kiss, of pulling away from Kelsey's embrace.

Maybe his battery would die. Maybe the signal would cut out.

His wishes went unheard as the phone rang again. Desire gradually clearing from her eyes as her breathing slowed, Kelsey pushed at his shoulders, and he had no choice but to back away.

"It's not important," he vowed, hoping his words were true as he fumbled with the phone. "I'll turn it off." He actually had his thumb on the button when he saw the number glowing on the small screen, and hesitated.

Just a split second, but the slight pause didn't get by Kelsey. "Who is it?"

The husky, passion-filled sound of her voice sent another shaft of desire straight to his gut. He could still turn the phone off. Turn it off and pretend the interruption had never taken place. The lie hovered in his thoughts, but meeting her gaze, he couldn't take the easy way out. "It's Emily."

Kelsey's eyes widened, and the warmth in them chilled even as the fire in her cheeks suddenly blazed. "Well, then, you should answer it."

"Kelsey—"

"Answer the phone, Connor."

Biting back a curse, he nearly barked into the phone, "Yeah?"

"Connor…is that you?"

"It's me. What's up?" Silence followed the brusque demand, and wouldn't it figure if the damn signal cut out *now.* "Em? You still there?"

"Yes. I'm here. What are you— Never mind. You sound like you're busy."

Forcing the slang definition of *busy* from his thoughts, he cleared his throat and asked, "What's wrong?"

"Nothing, really. Can't I call without you assuming something's wrong?"

A note of desperation had entered her voice, telling Connor it was more than an assumption. "Yeah, sure you can. So, what's up?"

"I guess I wanted to talk," she offered, uncertainty filling her voice.

Connor couldn't help glancing over at Kelsey. Her face turned away from him, she was determinedly ignoring the conversation going on only a cushion away.

Hesitation cost him for the second time in a matter of minutes when Emily said, "This was a bad idea. I shouldn't have called."

"Em—" The line went silent before he could come up with even a halfhearted protest. Flipping the phone closed, he slid the tiny device back in his pocket.

"What did she say?"

"Not much."

"She didn't say why she called?"

"No." And he didn't care. At least, not nearly as much as he cared about what was going through Kelsey's mind. "Kelsey—"

"It's okay."

"Really?" Connor asked, doubt lacing the word.

But when Kelsey met his gaze, a smile teased her lips. A little shaky around the edges, but a smile just the same. And Connor felt something in his heart catch at her remarkable strength and resiliency. He knew the call had to bring up reminders of his relationship with Emily as well as Kelsey's long-ingrained feelings of inferiority.

"Really," she insisted. "Like you said, we can't change the past, and I think it's time we both moved on."

Chapter Nine

"Kelsey, this is a surprise." Emily rose from the large oak table in her parents' kitchen, where she'd been flipping through a bridal magazine, and gave her a hug.

"I had a free morning and wanted to come by and invite you to breakfast." Kelsey mentally cringed at the half-truth. She *did* have a free morning, but the invitation was an excuse to find out what that phone call to Connor meant.

Emily wrinkled her nose. "I can't. I'll never fit into my wedding dress if I stuff myself with waffles."

So Emily was still dieting. Almost every bride thought about dieting before the big day even if they didn't stick with it. Or need to lose a single pound, Kelsey thought, as Emily walked over to the pantry—slender, graceful, and gorgeous. A powder-blue silk robe wrapped her body, and her hair was pulled back in a simple ponytail.

"You can keep me company while I have some tea and toast," her cousin suggested, a hopeful note coming to her voice.

"I'd love to. It'll give us a chance to talk."

After setting a kettle on the stove, Emily popped a piece of what looked like whole-wheat cardboard into the toaster. "What did you want to talk about?" she asked, once Kelsey declined her offer of toast in favor of fresh strawberries.

About that phone call last night, Kelsey thought. *The one you placed an hour after your oh-so-perfect fiancé met a Realtor at your dream house.*

"Uh…" Unable to jump into the conversation, her mind blanked and the last thing she expected popped out of her mouth. "I saw Matt the other night."

"No!" Looking appropriately horrified and curious, Emily sank back against the tan-and-gold-flecked granite countertops. "What happened?" Before Kelsey could answer, Emily waved off the question. "No, don't start yet."

She plopped a tea bag in a mug the size of a cereal bowl, poured the hot water and dropped her hot toast—sans butter—onto a plate. Settling eagerly onto the chair next to Kelsey, she said, "Okay, tell me everything. Did he beg you to take him back? Has he come to his senses and realized that other woman can't compare to you?"

Kelsey managed a small smile, knowing Emily didn't realize the irony of her words. Kelsey had never told her cousin *she* was the woman Matt was in love with. As blind as Kelsey had been to her ex's infatuation, Emily had missed the signs, as well. Of course, she was used to attracting male attention. Matt's shy and awkward behavior had been nothing new.

"No, he didn't beg me to come back." Though some begging had been involved, she recalled with satisfaction, thinking of Matt pleading with her to call Connor off.

But it was the look in Connor's eyes when he'd touched

her cheek that stayed in her mind, replaying like the romantic comedies she enjoyed. Last night's kiss was another memory that played over and over, and unfortunately her mind didn't come with a handy remote. The images had flickered across her eyelids for hours.

She'd talked a good game last night, declaring the past over and done for both of them, but could it be that easy? Facing Emily on a day when her cousin looked gorgeous—as usual—and Kelsey felt tired and cranky and worn by comparison, could she really believe Connor was over Emily?

Waving the desert-dry toast, Emily decreed, "You're better off without Matt."

"Yeah, that's what—that's what I think, too."

"You're an amazing woman, Kelsey. You're sweet, successful. You own your own business, and you're so totally organized."

Rolling her eyes, Kelsey ignored the heat rising in her cheeks. "I don't know about amazing."

"Do you know how impressed Daddy was when you didn't take money from him to start your business?"

"I couldn't. Your parents have already done so much for me." And Kelsey had never forgotten that her father had gotten her mother pregnant—with her—in the hope of getting his hands on the Wilson fortune. She was *not* her father's daughter, and she flat-out refused to step anywhere near the tracks he'd left behind. "I couldn't take money from them. Your mother's referrals have been the real boost the business needed."

Referrals that hinged on Emily's wedding going off without a hitch.

You're going to be a success with or without Emily's wedding. Connor's words echoed in her mind. *A single setback won't stop you.*

He was right, Kelsey realized. Weddings Amour was her

calling, her dream, one she would fight for. One wedding was not going to make or break her business.

Just like her family's approval or disapproval would not make or break *her.* She was stronger than her cousin, and if Connor was right about Todd, Kelsey needed to do what she could to look out for Emily.

With the reminder in mind, Kelsey said, "Enough about me. What's Todd up to this morning? Why aren't you two lovebirds hanging out?"

"He and Daddy went golfing."

Golf. Kelsey had never understood the sport. Especially not during the summer when tee-off times were at the break of dawn. "I'm surprised you didn't go with them."

Emily, along with looking chic in linen capris and argyle print polo shirts, was an amazing golfer. She gave a soft laugh. "You know. Gentlemen only, ladies forbidden."

"Hmm." That long-ago restriction, the acronym that gave golf its name, might have something to do with Kelsey's aversion to the sport. "You probably would have beaten them. Which might be why they didn't invite you."

"Oh, I wouldn't have—" A soft blush lit Emily's cheeks, and she turned her attention to peeling the crust from her toast.

"Wouldn't what, Em? Play to win?" Between the abbreviation of her cousin's name and the challenge she'd issued, Kelsey felt like a ventriloquist's dummy with Connor pulling the strings and his words coming out of her mouth. But as worried as she might be by his influence, her cousin's possible answer worried her more.

"Come on, Kelsey," Emily said, "you know how fragile the male ego can be."

"I can understand why you wouldn't want to show Todd up, but do you really want to live your life playing second best?"

"It's only a silly game of golf, Kelsey."

"I think it's more than that."

Emily's smile faded away, and Kelsey felt like she'd caught a glimpse of the real woman lost behind the beautiful facade. "Todd is a wonderful man. I love him. Really, I do, and I can't wait until we're married."

Kelsey had heard the words before, but this was the first time she sensed a touch of desperation underscoring the refrain. "Emily—" she began, but the opening of the kitchen door interrupted what she might have said.

"Kelsey, good morning," Charlene greeted Kelsey with raised eyebrows that seemed to ask why she wasn't keeping an eye on Connor as she'd been told. "I didn't expect to see you here."

Emily flashed a smile she'd perfected years ago, during her beautiful baby and pageant days. The slight tilt of her head, the perfect curve to her lips, the flash of white teeth. The smile was camera ready, but like an image captured on photo paper, it wasn't real. The moment and whatever else they might have said was gone.

"Kelsey came by to talk about the shower tomorrow and go over a few last-minute wedding details," she filled in, but the excuse only made Charlene frown.

"What details?"

"We're, um, we're going over the items Emily will carry down the aisle. You know, the something borrowed, something blue…"

"That's already decided, remember?" Charlene filled her own teacup and set the pot back on the stove. "You'll wear my pearls as something borrowed. I wore them at my wedding, and Aileen wore them at hers. It's tradition."

"Oh, right," Emily agreed. Kelsey knew her cousin thought pearls old-fashioned. Instead of making a fuss, though, Emily bowed to her mother's wishes. An argument built inside Kelsey like the steam building in the teapot, but what good would it do to stand up for her cousin when Emily wouldn't stand up for herself? "My bouquet will be tied with a blue ribbon, and my ring is new. So that leaves something old."

"I have a lace handkerchief that belonged to your great-grandmother." Adding a tea bag to the water, Charlene said, "Kelsey, run upstairs, would you? The handkerchief is in the bottom drawer of my dresser."

Charlene turned back to the counter to add sugar to her tea, and Kelsey wondered if her aunt was sending her on the errand because she didn't want to leave Emily and Kelsey alone. Still, she agreed. "I'll go get it."

During the years Kelsey had lived with her aunt and uncle, she rarely intruded on their sanctuary. Once she stepped inside, she saw the dresser had three bottom drawers. Which one would hold the handkerchief Charlene mentioned?

Kelsey started at the nearest drawer and found a collection of family mementos. Glancing through the items, she realized these were her uncle's belongings, not her aunt's. A packet of envelopes nestled among a worn-out glove and baseball cap. She slid the drawer halfway closed before she noticed the address on the top envelope. A Nevada location that had once been her home.

Hesitating, she reached for the letters. Kelsey flipped through one after the other, noting the changing addresses and postmark dates as well as the undeniable "return to sender" printed across the fronts.

"You can open them if you want."

Kelsey jumped at the sound of her uncle's voice. Gordon stood framed by the doorway. Dressed in tan slacks and a blue polo shirt, he looked more casual than usual. The hint of sunburn above his close-cropped beard told of the morning hours spent on the golf course, and his silver-blond hair had recently lost some of its structured style. But regardless of what he wore, her uncle was a tall, handsome man whose presence demanded attention and respect.

Clutching the letters to her chest, she said, “Aunt Charlene sent me to look for Great-grandmother’s handkerchief. For the wedding. You know, something old—”

Gordon waved a hand. “The middle drawer is your aunt’s.”

Ignoring the errand that had sent her to the room, Kelsey held out the letters. “You wrote to my mother?”

Gordon nodded. “More times than I can count. But it was all too little, too late.”

Too little. Kelsey flipped through the envelopes—years’ worth of envelopes, years’ worth of effort—seeing nothing little about it. “I don’t understand.”

“Your grandfather was a hard man. He wouldn’t stand for any sign of defiance, and your mother—” Gordon shook his head with a bittersweet smile. “Your mother challenged him from the day she was born. They butted heads constantly, but when she refused to stop seeing your father, that was an impasse neither of them could cross.”

Kelsey’s hands tightened on the letters at the mention of her father. “Maybe she should have listened.”

“She made a bad choice, and at the time I thought your grandfather handled the situation very poorly. Years later I realized how desperate he must have felt to make the ultimatum he did—forcing your mother to choose between her family and your father.”

And her mother chose Donnie Mardell. She’d never talked about him, and not until her illness reached a point where there was no hope did she tell Kelsey the whole story. How she had defied her father to leave home with Donnie. How her father refused to accept that decision and paid Donnie to leave town, thinking that would force Olivia to come to heel.

But that plan backfired. Donnie left town, money burning

a hole in his pocket, but Olivia hadn't returned home. Instead, she fled even farther, cutting all contact with her family…to the point where Kelsey hadn't known she *had* any family.

Regret furrowed his forehead. "I'd hoped your mother could forgive me for what she saw as my decision to side with our father." Gordon shook his head. "So stubborn, the both of them. So unwilling to bend."

Instant denial rose up inside Kelsey. "My mother was brave and strong. She took care of herself and me without help from *anyone.*"

"And she raised you to do the same, didn't she?"

Kelsey opened her mouth to respond, only to be silenced by her mother's voice echoing in her mind. *You may not have been raised as one of the wealthy Wilsons, but you're better than they are. Hold your head high and prove to them what an amazing young woman I've raised.*

She'd done her best, trying to prove herself instead of simply *being* herself. All the judgments, all the expectations, had her aunt and uncle put them on Kelsey…or had Olivia with her dying words?

Lifting a hand, Gordon brushed his fingertips against the edges of the envelopes, flipping through fifteen years of unanswered pleas. "She was my only sibling. The last link to my childhood and my parents. I never stopped hoping we'd have the chance to overcome the differences of the past. But she was so determined to prove she didn't need anybody." He met Kelsey's gaze with a melancholy grin. "There's no doubt *you* are your mother's daughter."

She'd spent eight years trying to be exactly that. Struggling to prove herself by trying to follow step by humiliating step in her cousins' footprints rather than simply *telling* her aunt and uncle she wasn't cut out for ballet or dressage or the lead role in the school play. Insisting on taking summer jobs to pay for her clothes and books and CDs; refusing to accept her uncle's loan to get her business going.

How many other times had she pushed her aunt and uncle away in her desperation to live up to her mother's stubborn independence? Unlike Olivia, Kelsey hadn't been totally alone, but she *had* followed her mother's footsteps when it came to protecting her heart. She'd kept people at a distance, never letting anyone—even family—too close, so she could never be let down, never be disappointed. Even with Matt...Kelsey saw now she'd purposely picked someone she liked but could never love.

And what about Connor? Had she resisted because she was afraid of his lingering feelings for Emily...or simply because she was afraid? Was she using his past as an excuse the same way her mother had held Gordon's past decisions against him? A reason not to give him—not to give *anyone*—a second chance?

Wilson women against the world. The motto that had once been a battle cry of strength and independence now seemed a cowardly whimper. And an excuse not to trust, not to fall in love...

Swallowing the lump in her throat, she asked, "Why didn't you tell me? Why let me think you'd cut my mother out of your life like your father did?"

Sorrow for the sister he'd lost pulled at Gordon's features. "Olivia was gone, and I didn't want to make you choose between your memory of her—your *good* memories of her—and the truth I could have told you."

Kelsey wondered if she might have been better off knowing the truth, but how could she fault her uncle when he'd made such an unselfish decision? "I'm so sorry, Uncle Gordon."

"Don't be. I know how much your mother meant to you, and I'd never want to take that away. Besides, I'm proud of you, Kelsey. Of your determination and drive. I'm sure your mother would be, as well."

Kelsey tried to answer, but the words were blocked by the lump in her throat. Swallowing, she said, "Uncle Gordon—"

"Kelsey, can't you find the handkerchief?" Charlene entered the bedroom and stepped around her husband. She frowned at the drawer Kelsey had left open. Her heart skipped a beat as her aunt crossed the room. But Charlene merely pushed the drawer shut, opened the correct one and lifted the handkerchief without sparing the envelopes in Kelsey's hand a single glance.

"Here it is," she said with an exasperated sigh. "I might as well hold on to it."

Kelsey blinked, the past falling away as she refocused on the present. "Isn't Emily downstairs?"

"Todd invited her to brunch."

She'd missed her chance to talk to Emily about her feelings for Todd and about the wedding, but Kelsey couldn't think about anything but the letters in her hands.

"Speaking of brunch," Gordon said, "I'm starved. You wouldn't believe the calories I burned beating that future son-in-law of mine. Although I do think he might have let me win."

"Nonsense," Charlene said briskly. "Experience trumps youth every time."

"I, um, should go," Kelsey said, ducking past her aunt. She tried to slip her uncle the letters, but he squeezed her hands and mouthed, "Keep them."

After giving a brief nod, Kelsey jogged down the stairs with her uncle's written words in her hands and his voice in her head.

You are your mother's daughter.

Connor stepped out of the shower, dropped the damp towel onto the marble floor in a limp heap and seriously considered following suit himself. He couldn't remember the last time he'd done enough reps to leave his arms and legs flopping like fish out of water.

His cell phone beeped as he pulled on a pair of well-worn jeans. The sound immediately took him back to the evening before and the reason he'd needed the killer workout. Memories of Kelsey's kiss, the feel of her curves beneath his hands, and the untimely interruption had tortured him through the night.

Only, the sound wasn't alerting him to an incoming call, but to a new message. Seeing Jake's number on the screen, he quickly dialed his voice mail.

"Come on, Jake. Tell me Sophia Pirelli gave you something on Dunworthy," he muttered while he waited for the message to play.

"Whatever happened to Sophia in Chicago still has her feeling vulnerable," Jake's message announced without preamble. "I'm getting close, though. She—she's starting to trust me. It won't be long now."

His friend said the words with an almost grim sense of finality. Once Jake found out what had made Sophia quit her job and whether or not it had anything to do with Dunworthy, Jake would be on the next plane back to L.A.

Just as Connor would be leaving Scottsdale…leaving Kelsey…

Leaving Kelsey to pick up the pieces, he thought as he snapped the phone shut and tossed it back on the dresser. If Emily called off the wedding, would it ruin Kelsey's business? He'd told her she had the strength and determination to succeed no matter what, and while he'd meant every word, he really didn't know what the hell he was talking about, did he? Could her dreams end up buried beneath a landslide of bad publicity for a wedding gone wrong?

And what about her family? The Wilsons were counting

on Kelsey. Would she see her failure as yet another time when she hadn't lived up to expectations?

But what was he supposed to do? Connor wondered. Step back and let Emily marry a guy with a narcissistic streak running like a fault line beneath his charming, sophisticated facade? Raise a glass of champagne and hope for the best?

Cara Mitchell would likely be dead if not for you. You saved her life, Connor.

He still wasn't sure he could take credit instead of blame for what happened to Cara, but he did know he couldn't have walked away. Just like he couldn't walk away from Emily.

But maybe he needed to walk away from Kelsey…

Bad enough that he'd be leaving her to deal with the professional fallout. The last thing he wanted was to leave her personal life in shambles after an affair that wouldn't—couldn't—go anywhere. It would be best to end things now, before someone got hurt.

Are you so sure it's Kelsey *you're trying to protect?* his sarcastic inner voice questioned, mocking his noble intentions for what they were—the act of a coward.

When it came right down to it, he had his own heart to protect, too. And Kelsey—with her caring, her concern, her willingness to see the best in everyone, including him—was already way too close to working her way inside.

A quiet knock on the door broke into his thoughts. He didn't bother to check the keyhole, accustomed to being able to handle anything, only to open the door and realize he could still be caught off guard.

Kelsey stood in the hallway, a lost look on her face.

"What are you doing here?" The question bordered on rude, but as he took in the uncertainty in her wide brown eyes, the sexier-than-hell freckles on her pale face, the plump lower lip she held caught between her teeth, his earlier intentions blew up in his face.

Walk away? As he caught the cinnamon scent of her skin, he couldn't even *move.*

"I went to see Emily this morning," she said as she ducked through the doorway. "I wanted to find out why she called you last night."

Last night.

The two simple words had the power to turn back time. His flesh still burned in the aftermath of her touch. He grabbed a clean T-shirt from the dresser and jerked it over his head as if he could smother the memories. Not likely. It would take much stronger fabric than simple cotton, especially with Kelsey standing mere feet from his bed.

Pushing his damp hair back with both hands, he caught Kelsey staring at him, desire and awareness swirling in her chocolate eyes. Slowly lowering his arms, he shoved his hands into the back pockets of his jeans rather than pull her into his arms. As if sensing his thoughts, Kelsey broke eye contact, her gaze skittering away as soft color lit her cheeks.

In a voice that sounded dry as the desert, he asked, "Did you?"

Blinking like waking from a dream, Kelsey asked, "Did I what?"

"Find out why Em called?"

"No. Well, maybe. It sounds like Uncle Gordon and Todd are getting pretty close. Emily says she's happy about it, but I'm not so sure."

Connor nodded. "Makes sense. Emily's always wanted her father's approval, and she's never known how to get it."

Silence followed his statement. He wasn't sure when he lost Kelsey. Her gaze was focused on the far wall, and he doubted she was captivated by the desertscape watercolor.

"Kelsey? You okay?"

"All this time, I thought I knew, but it was a lie, and I can't ask her why."

He frowned. "Ask who what?"

Shaking her head, she came back from whatever place or time had her spellbound. "Sorry. You don't even know what I'm talking about." She clutched at the oversize purse hanging from her shoulder, the lost, almost haunted look coming back.

Concern accomplished what little else could—pushing desire to the back burner. He stepped closer and watched her throat move as she swallowed—thanks to whatever she must have seen in his eyes—but he merely took her hand and led her to the couch.

"Tell me," he urged. "Maybe I can figure it out."

"If you can, you're one up on me," she said with a sound that could have been a laugh but wasn't. Still, she took a deep breath as she sank against one of the cushions and said, "Aunt Charlene walked in when I was with Emily. We told her we'd been discussing what Emily would carry down the aisle. Something old, something new…"

Kelsey seemed to expect him to fill in the rest, so Connor ventured, "Roses are red, violets are blue?"

A slight smile tweaked her lips, and she said, "Close. Something borrowed, something blue." Her smile faded as she pulled a rubber-banded stack of envelopes out of her purse. "I went looking for something old."

"And you found those?" he asked, nodding at the bundle in her hands.

"These are letters my uncle wrote to my mother. Letters I never knew about. From an uncle I never knew existed until I was sixteen."

Slowly Kelsey filled Connor in about her wrong-side-of-the-tracks father, about the demand her grandfather had made of her mother, and the money he'd paid her father to leave.

The words were a sucker punch to Connor's soul. "Your grandfather paid your father off?"

Damned if he didn't have to give the family credit. They were consistent if not original. Clearly payoffs were standard practice when it came to getting rid of unwanted boyfriends. He still remembered the look on Gordon Wilson's face when the older man handed *him* a check to stay away from Emily.

Money he still hadn't told Kelsey about…

"He took the money and never looked back. He didn't care that my mother gave up everything for him. Didn't even care that she was pregnant with me."

An old bitterness, stale and rusty, cut into Kelsey's words, and panic started to grow inside Connor. "But if he never contacted your mother, then you don't know his reasons. You don't know why he took the money—"

Kelsey gave a scoffing laugh. "Oh, believe me. I know *why.* He took the money because he was a selfish bastard. It was all he was interested in, all he wanted, and as soon as it was his, he was gone. Nothing he could say would matter, nothing he could do would ever make up for taking the money."

She might as well be talking about him, Connor thought, guilt churning inside him. There was nothing he could do to change the past. He'd known when he took the money, Emily would never understand why he'd done it, why it was so vital that he help the Delgados. Would Kelsey really be any different?

She is *different,* his conscience argued.

And, yeah, okay, he'd taken her to meet Maria with the thought that he could somehow explain. But with her past and her father's bought-and-paid-for desertion, well, she'd it said herself, hadn't she?

Nothing he could say would matter…

"I'm sorry, Kelsey," he bit out. Sorry for reasons he couldn't even tell her.

"So am I," she said as she placed the letters on the coffee table. Taking a deep breath, she seemed to come to a decision as she turned on the couch cushion to face him. "I'm sorry my mother couldn't see another choice—to let go of the past. But I've been just as guilty."

"Kelsey—"

"It's true," she insisted. "I've always kept my aunt and uncle at a distance. You saw that. I was afraid to trust them, to count on them, in case they turned their backs on me the same way I thought they'd turned their backs on my mom."

"And Gordon never told you the whole story until now?"

Kelsey shook her head. "He said he didn't want to make me choose between my loyalty to my mom and them." She caught sight of Connor's surprised look and added, "See? He's not all bad."

Surprising her, Connor said, "Yeah, I'm starting to see that." His jaw clenched. "I mean, talk about the past repeating. He looked at me and saw a guy like your father—"

"You're nothing like him," Kelsey insisted fiercely.

"Kelsey, you don't know—"

"I do. I know you're a good man."

A pained expression crossed his face. "No."

"You are," she insisted.

She thought of the way he'd taken responsibility for the women in his life: his mother, Emily, Cara Mitchell. He'd saved the woman's life, yet he held himself accountable for putting her in a dangerous situation. Then, there was the love and gratitude he showed the Delgados. And yet none of those things compared to how he made her feel. She didn't want to be a responsibility. She certainly didn't want to be family. She wanted to be the woman Connor thought she was—strong, beautiful, sexy…

She did not want to be her mother's daughter, refusing to give or take second chances. And while Connor had never actually *told* her she was sexy, he gave her the confidence to believe she was. Taking a deep breath, the emotions that had been swirling through her calmed, settled, focused on the present, on this moment, and what she wanted. "And I might be my mother's daughter, but I don't have to live my life like she did."

The confusion clouding Connor's expression dispersed as Kelsey rose to her knees and leaned closer. Crystal-clear desire and equally obvious denial filled the void. "Kelsey, wait."

Determined to wipe that denial from his eyes, Kelsey swung her knee over Connor's thighs. He caught her around the waist, the heat in his gaze burning brighter as his fingers flexed into her hips. Instead of pulling her closer, he held her steady. "Kelsey, you don't know—"

His hesitation only pushed Kelsey forward. "I know I want you to kiss me."

One kiss was all it would take to bury her doubts in a flood of need. She should have known Connor wouldn't make it that easy on her. Or on himself. A war seemed to rage inside him, the frown between his eyebrows and the lines cutting grooves in his cheeks telling the tale of the battle.

One she thought she might win when his gaze dropped to her mouth. His voice a husky rasp, he asked, "That's all you want? A kiss?"

Almost unconsciously she licked her lips, a feminine thrill rushing through her when she saw his eyes darken with desire. "It's a good place to start, don't you think?"

And she could think of only one place she wanted to finish—in Connor's arms and in his bed, with no phone calls or memories of the past to interfere. Reaching up to trace the planes and angles of his face, from the doubt still pulling at his eyebrows to the tension locking his jaw, her cousin Aileen's words rang in her head.

Connor's the kind of man who makes a woman want to live for the moment.

Maybe that was true, but all she wanted was this man, in this moment, Kelsey insisted, ignoring the greedy voice demanding more…demanding forever.

"Now," she argued with that voice, "I just want now."

"Want what?" Connor demanded, his voice a rough scrape that sent shivers down her nerve endings.

"This," she whispered as she brushed her fingertips over his mouth. "You."

Her pulse pounded so wildly in her ears, Kelsey barely heard the words, but to Connor, her response must have been loud and clear. The one word broke through his hesitation. Leaning forward, he pulled her tighter and caught her lips in the kiss she'd waited for. Just like she'd hoped, the sheer pleasure of his mouth on hers banished all doubt, erasing any worries about anything…or anyone.

His hands still on her hips, he twisted to the side, lowering her to the couch without breaking the mind-spinning kiss. She sank into the cushions, Connor's weight pressing her deeper, but even the full-body contact wasn't enough. She ran her hands down his back, breathing in his fresh-from-the-shower scent. Breaking the kiss, she trailed her lips down the column of his throat. His skin was still slightly damp, and she sipped tiny droplets of water from his skin like a woman dying of thirst in the desert.

And maybe she was, Kelsey thought, vaguely surprised by the need and desire spurring her on. After all, it had been a *long* time…

Rising on an elbow, Connor levered away from her. For a split second, Kelsey worried that something—the hotel room, the couch, *something*—had reminded him of the past, of Emily, and that he was going to pull away and leave her wanting. But neither the past nor, heaven forbid, Emily were reflected in his eyes. Instead, Kelsey saw herself as he saw her, and for the first time in her life, she felt beautiful.

"Connor." His name broke from her in a shaky whisper. She didn't think she could speak another word if she tried, but he said everything she wanted to say…everything she wanted to hear.

"A kiss is never going to be enough. I want more. I want everything."

"Okay," she breathed.

Connor's lips quirked in a half smile. "Okay?"

Nodding fiercely, she repeated, "Okay."

Taking her at her word, as limited as it might have been, Connor reclaimed her lips in a teasing, tantalizing kiss even as his fingers toyed with the buttons on her shirt. But after his determined comment, Kelsey should have known Connor wasn't playing.

Before she was even aware of what happened, Connor's hot palm laid claim to the bare skin of her stomach, stealing her breath from the outside in as Kelsey realized he'd completely unbuttoned her shirt.

"Amazing," he murmured, his eyes taking the curves rising and falling with every rapid breath.

Glancing at the off-white, no-frills bra, she gave a short laugh. She hadn't gone to Connor's hotel with seduction in mind and it showed. "Boring," she argued.

"Are you kidding?" Tracing a path across the freckles on her chest, a focused, concentrated frown on his face, Connor vowed, "I think I just found a map to the Lost Dutchman's mine."

The silly comment startled a laugh from Kelsey, and Connor's touch veered closer to hitting a different kind of gold mine. His fingers followed the map work of freckles, and her laughter faded away. Breathless anticipation took over, and she arched into his touch.

The plain material proved no match for Connor. He reached inside to cup her breast, and her nipple instantly tightened against his palm. The sheer pleasure of his touch sent her head spinning, and each gasp for breath only pressed her flesh tighter into his hand. He kissed her again, and Kelsey welcomed the exploring quest of his tongue. Her hands searched for the hem of his shirt, seeking out hidden treasure for herself. She followed the plain of his back, the valley of his spine, the rise of his shoulder blades, but none of it was enough.

Pulling her mouth away from his, she gasped, "Connor, wait."

"What's wrong?" Despite the desire pinpointing his pupils and turning his voice to gravel, Connor followed her command. Other than the rapid rise and fall of his chest, he didn't move a muscle.

And Kelsey couldn't help smiling. "You didn't want to make out in a car, and I don't want to make love on a couch. Not when the bed is only a few feet away."

Eyes dark with desire, he accused, "I told you, you make me crazy."

"The feeling's mutual."

Connor pushed off the couch and held out a hand. She linked her fingers through his and clung tight, desperate to hold onto the moment. But unlike previous interruptions that broke the mood, the walk to the bedroom, amid heated kisses and arousing touches, heightened the intensity. Her fingers clumsy with haste, Kelsey tugged at Connor's T-shirt. She stopped kissing him only long enough to push the shirt over his head and toss it aside.

In the back of her mind, she was still slightly amazed by her own actions. For the first time, need overwhelmed nerves. She could have blamed the previous interruptions or her own personal dry spell for the undeniable hunger. But the real reason was Connor. All Connor…

He pushed her shirt from her shoulders, then stripped away her bra, and Kelsey let the garments fall, too fascinated by the sheer perfection of his broad shoulders, muscular chest and flat stomach to care about the imperfection of freckles dotting her skin. Especially not when Connor seemed so fascinated by connecting the random marks and turning them into shapes: stars, triangles, hearts…

But the arousing touch was nothing compared to the intensity of his lips as they charted that same course. The damp heat of his breath against her skin was like a promise, and when his mouth made good on that promise, Kelsey's knees went weak. Connor followed her down to the mattress and reached for the waistband of her skirt. She expected him to whisk it away as quickly as he had her shirt, but instead her skirt and panties made a slow slide down the length of her legs. Inch by inch, and by the time he slipped them off, Kelsey had never been so glad to be so short.

"Connor." His name broke from her in a plea, and his green eyes glittered as he ran his hand up the inside of her thigh.

"Definitely not boring," he murmured. He stroked her skin, and waves of pleasure washed over her. She cried out his name a second time, even as he shoved aside his jeans. The well-worn denim did not make the same slow journey as her skirt. He kicked the jeans aside in a split second, then braced his body above hers.

He claimed her mouth in a kiss, his tongue plunging deep in the same moment he buried himself between her thighs. Her back arched, her body rising to meet his, and his low groan of desire escaped their kiss. And this time it was her name that broke the silence as Connor caught her hips in his hands.

That first thrust was like the striptease with her skirt: slow, seductive, measured. But then urgency took over, reckless and wild, and Kelsey had the instant thought that this must be what it was like to ride on the back of a bike—amazed, exhilarated and desperate to hold on. But unlike on a bike, the real ride began when she lost control, careening riotously, hurtling down a path that ended in a fiery explosion as she shuddered in ecstasy a second time, bringing Connor with her.

They collapsed in a heap together, both trying to catch their breath. "Definitely not boring," Connor repeated, as he brushed the hair away from her face. The look of tenderness in his gaze brought an ache to her throat, and Kelsey was glad when Connor eased away and tucked her against his side before he saw the tears burning her eyes.

With her head on his chest, Kelsey listened to his heartbeat gradually slow. But even without the weight of his body on hers, she couldn't breathe. A relentless pressure squeezed her heart, like she'd dived too deep and realized too late how far she was in over her head.

Her first impression had been wrong. Connor wasn't the type of man who made a woman want to live for the moment. He was the type of man, the *only* man, who'd made Kelsey long for forever.

Chapter Ten

Connor woke slowly, aware of two things. First it was way too early, and second, Kelsey was no longer in bed. The low murmur of her voice pulled him the rest of the way from sleep. "Everything's all set, and I'll be there to oversee the decorations and food." A slight pause followed. "Must be a bad connection. I'm—outside. I'll run out and get the cake right before the guests arrive. Yes, I'll make sure to leave plenty of time. Can I talk to Emily for a second? Oh, right. Of course. She needs her beauty sleep. I'll see you in an hour. Okay. Forty-five minutes. Bye."

A narrow shaft of light sliced through the curtains, and in the muted glow he watched Kelsey slip on her shoes. He didn't move or make a sound, but something must have given him away. She stiffened slightly and glanced his way as she straightened. "Hey," she said softly. "I was trying not to wake you."

She pushed her hair behind her ear in a nervous gesture,

and Connor felt a flicker of annoyance. What was she going to do? Slip away while he was still sleeping? And why the hell would that bother him? It wasn't as if he hadn't done the same thing before. But that was before, and those women weren't Kelsey, and he didn't want her to go.

A knot twisted in his stomach at the thought of asking her to stay. The memory of his mother's sad smile as she walked away time and time again flashed in his mind, and the words jammed in his throat. He fisted his hands against the mattress and pushed into a sitting position with a glance at the clock. "It's not even seven."

Her gaze fell from his to land on his naked chest and then cut away to search out the purse she'd left on the couch, but not before he'd seen something in her eyes that made the knot in his stomach tighten.

"I know it's early, but Emily's shower is this morning, and I have to oversee the decorations and the food and— I'm sorry."

Connor wasn't sure why she was apologizing—for the early hour, for leaving, for Emily's shower…or for the regret he'd seen in her eyes.

He'd known Kelsey would regret sleeping with him, but he'd taken her at her word when she said she wanted him. He'd believed her because—hell, because he'd wanted to believe her. But that was last night. Now, in the full light of day, with the Charlene Wilson calling the shots, everything changed.

Or, he thought grimly, everything was the same. Only this time it was Kelsey lying to the Wilsons, sneaking behind their backs to see him. It was Kelsey who pretended her relationship with him didn't exist. Familiar ground, but it hurt a hell of a lot more the second time around. And not because she'd torn open old wounds. Emily had damaged his pride, but this—this felt like something else entirely.

Tossing aside the sheet in an obvious reminder that last

night *had* happened, Connor swung his legs over the edge of the mattress and stood. Some other time, he might have teased Kelsey about the blush blooming in her face. But not this morning. Not when the heat signaled a different kind of embarrassment. He jerked on his jeans as quickly as he'd stripped them off the night before, annoyed by his body's reaction to the mere thought.

"I'm going to talk to Emily about the wedding—"

"I don't give a damn about the wedding," he said, surprised by the truth of the words. He was still worried about Emily, but as far as proving the Wilsons wrong about Dunworthy, proving them wrong about *him,* Connor no longer cared. Only Kelsey's opinion mattered, an opinion suddenly in doubt.

"I'm sorry," she repeated, before lifting distraught eyes to his.

Yeah, he got that part. She was sorry they'd slept together.

"Last night was…"

Connor's jaw clenched, waiting for the word he *knew* was coming.

"…amazing, and I'd give anything to stay in bed with you—"

"Wait? What?"

"Last night was amazing." Color flared brighter, nearly blotting out her freckles as she ducked her head. "At least I thought it was, but I'm not—"

Swallowing a curse, Connor pulled her into his arms as realization hit him like the slap upside the head he deserved. Kelsey's reactions hadn't been fueled by regret or embarrassment but by a vulnerability that played against his own insecurities. "Last night *was* amazing."

The memory combined with Kelsey's soft curves pressed against him, her warm breath feathering across his chest, was enough to remind him just *how* amazing.

"It was," Kelsey whispered. He heard the relief in her voice, felt her smile against his skin.

"This morning could be even more amazing."

"I know." Despite the apparent agreement in her words, her smile fell away, and this time, he knew he wasn't imagining the regret in her voice. Pulling out of his arms, she said, "And that's why I have to go. Because whether you give a damn or not, Emily's wedding is a week away and then you'll be going home."

She was talking about L.A., but home didn't bring to mind images of his sterile apartment. Instead, he thought of Señora Delgado's restaurant, he thought of his friendship with Javy, and he thought of every moment he'd spent with Kelsey…and he wondered what might happen if he didn't go back to L.A.

"Kelsey—"

"So, see? I have to leave," she continued despite his interruption. "Last night was an amazing moment, but it wasn't meant to last, right?"

The hope in her eyes waited for him to contradict every word she'd said, to tell her sometimes amazing moments added up to a lifetime, but he couldn't make himself say the words.

Ducking her head, Kelsey grabbed her purse off the couch and left. And even though the sound of the closing door slammed into his chest like a blow, Connor let her go. Because when it came right down to it, he was the one too afraid to ask her to stay.

Connor didn't have a destination in mind when he climbed behind the Mustang's wheel, but he couldn't stay in the hotel room any longer. Fortunately, Javy's car seemed to have a mind of its own, and he soon turned into the Delgado parking lot.

The restaurant wouldn't open for hours yet, but Connor knew Maria would already be in the kitchen, stirring giant pots of tortilla soup and prepping food. He pulled around back, the crunch of gravel beneath the tires the only sound, a sharp contrast to the night he'd brought Kelsey here when music and laughter filled the sultry air.

A metallic glint caught his eye as he climbed from the car, and he spotted a motionless wind chime made from silverware. Despite his mood, Connor smiled as a memory came to him. Furious with Javy over some scrape he'd gotten into, Maria whacked the counter with a carved spoon. The aged wood splintered on contact, adding to his mother's anger, and she'd threatened Javy with the dire prediction that if the restaurant closed, it would be all his fault; after all, how could she cook without her favorite spoon?

The statement was a meaningless heat-of-the-moment comment that had come far too close to coming true years later. Not because of a broken spoon, but due to the expenses that followed Javy's father's illness and the fire that had nearly destroyed the kitchen.

A faint humming broke into his memories, and he found Maria standing at the counter, vegetables piled high in front of her, the quick, continuous motion of the knife a steady rhythm to the song she sang beneath her breath. The rustic Delgado family recipes went back for decades, but the remodeled kitchen was completely modern with its stainless-steel counters and appliances.

Maria's face lit as he stepped inside the kitchen. "Connor! This is a surprise."

"I wanted to apologize for taking off without saying goodbye the other night."

She waved aside his apology with a flick of her knife before starting in on a jalapeno pepper, but curiosity lit her eyes as she said, "You and your Kelsey were in a hurry, no?"

Her words wiggled like bait on a hook, but Connor didn't bite. His silence wasn't enough to make the *señora* pull in her line. Watching him from the corner of her eye, she added, "That is how it is when you are in love."

Love. The word sent a flare of panic scorching through him like the grease fire that nearly destroyed the restaurant years ago. "Kelsey and I aren't in love."

Maria glared at him like she might toss him back into the water. "I was married to my Miguel for over twenty years. I know love."

Connor knew love, too. He knew the pain of losing a mother who loved him yet left him no matter how many times he asked her to stay. He knew the heartache of losing Emily, who claimed to love him but not enough to defy her parents. And Kelsey…would loving her be any different? If he told her the truth about the money he'd taken, money he'd used to save the restaurant, would love be enough to make her understand? Would it be enough for her to stand up to the family who'd taken her in when she was sixteen and scared with nowhere else to go?

"You don't understand, Maria. Kelsey's a Wilson. She's Emily's cousin—"

"And you think Kelsey is a foolish girl like Emily? Unable to think or do for herself?"

"No, she's not like that at all. She's used to taking care of herself and the people around her." He'd seen that at her shop, in her concern for her friends. Friends who had Kelsey's complete loyalty. Friends who *deserved* that loyalty.

Connor tried to picture Lisa or Trey fitting in at a Wilson family gathering and couldn't. Just as he couldn't imagine Kelsey caring what the Wilsons thought or ever, *ever* turning her back on her friends. Kelsey might not have wanted to follow in her mother's footsteps, but the path had led Kelsey to be a strong, independent woman. A woman who knew her own mind and knew what she wanted.

Suddenly it didn't matter if the Wilsons admitted they've been wrong about Dunworthy. It didn't even matter if they admitted they'd been wrong about *him.* All he cared about now was proving Kelsey *right.* She believed in him, and last night she'd wanted *him.* Now it was up to Connor to tell her the truth about the money he'd taken from her family and convince her she wanted more than a moment, that he could give her more. It was up to him to convince her that, together, they could have forever.

Kelsey struggled through the front door of her aunt and uncle's house, a huge bouquet of pink and silver helium-filled balloons trailing behind her. The carved wooden doors swung shut, catching one of the balloons in the jamb. She jumped as the loud-as-a-gunshot *pop* guaranteed her arrival wouldn't go unannounced.

"Kelsey. I expected you half an hour ago."

Okay, so she wouldn't have snuck in unnoticed anyway. "Sorry, Aunt Charlene."

"Where have you been?"

"With Connor." The truth popped out before the words even formed in her head, and she couldn't imagine what possessed her to tell the truth.

His image flashed in her mind, and she knew exactly what possessed her. She'd seen the look in his eyes when he'd caught her on the phone with her aunt. When he caught her *lying* to her aunt. If she wasn't such a coward, she would have told the truth when it mattered.

Just like she would have stayed with Connor that morning, in his hotel room, in his bed, with the courage to believe they could turn one night into something more.

Disapproval cut into Charlene's features, and Kelsey knew her aunt didn't think Connor was good enough for a Wilson—

any Wilson—but she knew the truth. She didn't deserve Connor.

"You're wrong about him," she announced, certainty backing ever word. "Connor's a good man. He isn't here to ruin Emily's life. He's here because he's worried she's marrying a man she doesn't love to please *you*."

Her aunt didn't speak. Kelsey thought maybe her words had made a difference, at least given her aunt pause. But Charlene's gaze never wavered, and as the silence grew, Kelsey knew her aunt wasn't using the silence to consider what Kelsey said. She was using the silence to make Kelsey *reconsider* what she'd said.

But she wasn't going to back down.

It was time for both her aunt and uncle to realize Connor was a good man, not some troubled kid out to steal their daughter. And they needed to let Emily go. To let her live her own life and to stop using one youthful indiscretion to keep her in line.

"Do you really think I can't see what's going on?" her aunt questioned on a sigh. "Connor McClane is out to stop Emily's wedding, and he's using you to do it! Honestly, Kelsey, I expected you to know better."

"Connor isn't using me. He wouldn't do that. I understand why you'd have a hard time believing he cares for me after how crazy he was about Emily—"

"Oh, for goodness' sake, follow me." Without checking to see if Kelsey would obey, Charlene turned on a heel and strode down the hall into Gordon's study. Kelsey reluctantly followed. "Connor wasn't in love with Emily any more than he's…"

In love with you. Her aunt's unspoken words bounced off the darkly paneled walls, hanging in the room like the scent of Gordon's cigars.

"The only thing that man has ever worried about is

himself." Crossing the room to open a desk drawer, she pulled out a manila folder. "When your uncle kept this for proof, I always thought Emily would be the one we'd show it to."

"Proof of what?" Kelsey asked uneasily as Charlene fingered a small rectangle of paper. The letters her uncle had written her mother had been shock enough. What else did her aunt and uncle have stashed away in desks and dressers?

"Proof of the kind of man Connor McClane really is." Charlene gazed at Kelsey across the polished mahogany surface, her gaze reflecting a hint of sympathy. "He must be very convincing. Emily was sure he loved her."

Kelsey didn't have her cousin's certainty. Connor had never mentioned the word *love*. But then again, neither had she, and Kelsey could no longer deny her feelings. She was in love with Connor. For a moment, she imagined saying the words out loud and punctuating them with a bold exit. Not needing any proof of the man Connor was aside from the truth written in her heart. But she wasn't that strong.

"What is it?" she whispered.

"See for yourself." Charlene slid the paper across the table. Kelsey stepped closer. It was a check. She recognized her uncle's signature, his name and address printed on the top left, the zeros following the number in the small box off to the right. But it was the person the check had been made out to that froze her gaze. Her stomach, which had been tossing back and forth, sank.

"Why do you think Connor left all those years ago? He might not have had Emily, but believe me, he got what he wanted."

Her hand shaking, Kelsey reached out and turned the check over. Connor's name was sprawled across the endorsement line. She stared at the signature rather than meet her aunt's knowing gaze. "That was a long time ago. Connor isn't the same person anymore."

Ten thousand dollars. A lot of money, but not enough to make a dent in the family fortune. Had her father held out for more? Kelsey wondered. Even twenty-four years ago, ten thousand dollars didn't go far. Ten years ago, it wouldn't have bought a new car.

"Is that what he told you? That he's changed?" Her aunt's cultured voice didn't reflect even a hint of disparagement, but Kelsey heard it all the same.

"He was a kid back when he was seeing Emily." An orphaned kid from the wrong side of the tracks. Could she blame him for taking the money? He'd told her how he'd struggled after his mother died.

But he didn't tell you about the check, a worried voice protested. She'd told him about the money her father took to abandon her and her mother, and Connor never said a word.

"Let's look at the way he's changed. Ten years ago, he nearly ruined Emily's life by convincing her to run away from her family with him. Now he's back, and this time he's out to ruin her life by convincing her to run away from her fiancé with him."

"That's not true," Kelsey argued against the ache in her chest. "He's concerned about Emily. Just like I am. She's making a mistake by marrying Todd."

"If I were you, I wouldn't be worried about Emily *or* Todd. I'd be worried about Connor McClane."

Kelsey wasn't sure how she made it through the shower. Probably thanks to her aunt's attention to detail. By following Charlene's every instruction, Kelsey moved by rote. She arranged the flowers and decorations; she picked up the cake and double-checked the catered finger food. She walked the guests through the games—silly, irreverent, last-days-as-a-free-woman tributes—followed by opening gifts.

Even in her dazed state, Kelsey could guess what each package contained. After all, she'd helped with the bridal registry, and no one would dare step outside the approved gift list. No surprises, just as her aunt demanded.

Charlene planned for every contingency. Even Connor McClane, Kelsey thought, her heart catching as his signature seemed to flash in front of her eyes, written by an unseen hand.

"Thank you, Kelsey! It's beautiful." Emily held up a snow globe. Strains of the wedding march filled the room as sparkling "snow" fell on the bride and groom waltzing through a wedding wonderland.

Kelsey offered a weak smile. She'd bought the gift B.C.—Before Connor. She couldn't *not* give her cousin a gift, but she felt as uncertain about Emily and Todd as she now did about Connor.

Kelsey had started to believe him, to trust his gut, as he called it, but now she didn't know what to believe, and her own gut was pitifully silent. "You're welcome, Emily. I just want you to be happy."

Emily masked the flicker of doubt with a wedding-portrait smile. "I am happy, Kelsey. I'm getting married!"

A half an hour later, as the guests were leaving, Kelsey started collecting the plates and utensils, her movements automatic and unthinking. She blinked in surprise when her aunt laid a hand on her arm.

"The maid can get that, Kelsey."

"It's my job—"

"And we're your family." Her expression softened to a degree Kelsey had never witnessed. "You're a beautiful woman in your own right, Kelsey, and I'm sorry if I've made you feel less than my own daughters. But there's only one thing Connor McClane is interested in, and it's not true love."

* * *

Kelsey debated calling Connor, but the conversation wasn't one she wanted to have over the phone. Stopping by his hotel room was out of the question. She'd come alive in Connor's arms the night before, letting go of the past and all her insecurities. But seeing proof of the money he'd taken, the past was in painful jeopardy of repeating. The insecurities Connor lifted with his seductive words and intoxicating touch crashed back down, hitting harder than ever. Making her question if last night had been as amazing as she'd thought…

Kelsey hit the brakes a good twenty feet shy of her driveway. The black Mustang was parked at the sidewalk, the right front tire bumped up on the curb. Mirrored glasses shielding his eyes, Connor leaned against the hood.

Ready or not, she was going to have to confront him about the money he'd taken. It wasn't something *she* could pretend hadn't happened. Nerves jerked in her stomach, and she carefully eased her foot back on the gas, her car crawling the last block.

Connor grinned as she stepped out of the car, and aching or not, her heart still sped up as he approached. Maybe he had a reason, an explanation for taking the money.

And a reason for keeping the truth from her?

Kelsey could forgive something that happened ten years ago, but why hadn't he told her? Why did she have to face the shock of another family secret?

"Hey, I went by to see Señora Delgado. You have an open invitation, and she made me promise that next time, I'd actually let you stay and eat." Connor stuck his hands in the pockets of his jeans, a hint of uncertainty in his stride weakening her resolve as she wondered what else he'd talked to the older woman about.

"Connor—"

"She likes you," he added with a crooked smile, "but then, who wouldn't?" His smile fell away when she didn't respond, and he stripped off his glasses. Worry shone in his emerald eyes. "What's wrong?"

"Wrong?" Kelsey echoed with a broken laugh, the word far too simple to describe everything that had happened. Her decision to trust him, to *sleep* with him, to defend him to her aunt…only to find out he was just like her father.

It was a long time ago, her heart argued. *Maybe he had a good reason. Maybe—*

"Why didn't you tell me?"

"Tell you what?"

"The real reason you left all those years ago. Why didn't you tell me about the money?"

A muscle in Connor's jaw flinched as if she'd slapped him. Kelsey wasn't sure what she'd expected—excuses, denials—but she hadn't counted on the dead silence that followed her words. The sun beat down on them, magnifying the pain in her head. Cicadas in a neighbor's tree started to buzz, a low pitch that soon revved louder and louder, building like the hurt and anger inside Kelsey until she couldn't keep from lashing out.

"I *told* you about my father—about the money he took to leave my mother, and you never said a word! I trusted you, I believed in you, I—"

Love you, she thought, her heart breaking as Connor stoically withstood her verbal attack. If not for that very first flinch, she wouldn't have even known he was listening.

Surely if he had some reason, some justification for taking the money beyond pure and simple greed, he would tell her. He would say…*something, anything!* But silence—*guilty* silence—was Connor's only response.

"My aunt and uncle were right about you all along," she

whispered. Just as her grandfather had been right about her father. "They were right about everything."

At her words, Connor finally reacted. A cruel, calculating smile curved his mouth, and though Kelsey never would have thought green eyes could be cold, a chill touched her as his gaze iced over. He looked every inch the bad boy her aunt had warned her about less than two weeks ago. If only she'd listened.

"Congratulations, Kelsey. Your family must be so proud. Seems like you're a real Wilson after all."

Muttering a curse beneath his breath, Connor stalked over to the car. Despite the weight of restrained sobs pressing on her chest, Kelsey let him go. She might have lived her life under the misconception of her and her mom against the world, but Connor was just as deluded, believing it was always him against the Wilsons. This wasn't about her family; it was all on Connor and the secret he'd kept.

"Mama's right. You look like hell."

Ignoring his friend's voice, Connor didn't look away from the production of sliced limes, saltshaker and shot glass he'd filled with tequila. He'd taken over the small outdoor bar at the back of the Delgados' restaurant, where they'd installed patio seating for times when the weather was nice. In the middle of June, even at eight o'clock at night, it wasn't.

He barely noticed the oppressive heat, the way his T-shirt clung damply to his skin, or the bugs that hovered around the string of multicolored lights. After shaking out salt on the back of his hand like it was rocket science, he reached for the shot glass.

Catching Connor's wrist, Javy asked, "How many of those have you had?"

Connor glared at his friend from the corner of his eye. "Counting this one? Two."

His friend barked out a laugh that ended in a curse as he let go. "You're in worse shape than I thought. Wanna tell me what happened?"

Wincing at the strong burn of the tequila, Connor replied, "You said it yourself when I brought Kelsey here. Some people never learn."

"Sorry, man."

Javy didn't say more, and the two of them sat without speaking. Mariachi music, the din of the diners, and the occasional shout from the kitchen were the only sounds.

Finally Connor shoved the shot glass aside. "It was Emily all over again. I was stupid enough to think things would be different this time. But when push came to shove, she sided with her family."

He'd seen the disappointment in Kelsey's eyes. Forget all she'd said about how he'd changed. Forget all they'd shared. She'd been waiting all along for him to show his true colors, and she'd jumped back to her own side of the tracks the minute his character came into question.

You should have told her sooner, his conscience berated him. If she hadn't found out the truth from Charlene… But would that have made a difference? Or would Kelsey's reaction have been the same?

He should have known he and Kelsey didn't have any chance at a future. Her family's disapproval would eat like acid, weakening Kelsey's feelings until they were worn clean away. He was lucky it had happened sooner rather than later. He couldn't stand to live life with Kelsey the way he had with his mother, always knowing she had one foot out the door and it was only a matter of time before she left and didn't come back.

"Wanna tell me what happened?"

"Her aunt told her I took money to leave town, to leave Emily."

"And she believed it?" his friend demanded, slumping back against the bar stool in disbelief. "Just like that? With no proof, no—"

"The Wilsons had all the proof they needed. I took the ten thousand dollars."

Shock straightened his friend's spine. "You what? But why would you—" Realization slowly spread across his features, along with a large dose of guilt. Javy swore. "Is that where you got the money you gave my mother for the restaurant?"

"Like you said, this place means everything to Maria. I couldn't let her lose it." Eyeing his friend closely, Connor said, "You never asked where I got the money."

"No, I never did." Javy let out a deep breath, reached for the bottle of tequila and poured himself a shot. For a long moment he stared into the glass before looking Connor in the eye. "I didn't want to know."

"What? In case I'd broken the law? Done something illegal?" Connor pressed. Well, why wouldn't Javy believe that? It was just the kind of thing Connor McClane would have done.

Once.

"You think *I* didn't consider it?" Javy shot back. "It's *my* restaurant! My responsibility. My family—"

"Mine, too."

"Yeah," his friend agreed, frustration and anger draining away. "But I should have been the one to come up with a solution. And you shouldn't be the one paying for it now."

"I made my choice, and I would do the same thing again. In a heartbeat. So, tell me, you gonna drink that?" Connor asked, pointing at the shot glass sitting untouched between them.

Javy slid it across the bar without spilling a drop. "Look, man, I've been trying to pay you back for years. You've gotta let me—"

"Forget it. After all your family did for me, it was the least I could do."

"Then we'll draw something up. Make you a partner in the restaurant. And I'll talk to Kelsey."

Connor shook his head. "No."

"What do you mean 'no'?" Javy demanded. "Why don't you want to tell her the truth?"

"She knows the truth. I took the money."

"Oh, come on, Connor! That's not the whole truth, and you damn well know it! If you told her *why,* Kelsey would understand."

Yeah, maybe she would…this time. But what about the next time she had to choose between him and her family?

Chapter Eleven

It had been three days since Kelsey had seen Connor. Three heartbreaking, regret-filled, uneventful days.

At first she'd been too hurt to do more than curl up on her sofa and cry. But Kelsey never believed self-pity helped anyone, so by the second day she had thrown herself into working on her shop, finishing up the details that transformed the place from a simple suite into the office of her dreams.

She'd had photographs from previous weddings enlarged and wrapped in gilded frames: an elegant wedding cake with a single piece missing; a bridal bouquet in midair with ribbons streaming; a close-up of an unseen couple's hands, fingers entwined, showing off sparkling wedding rings.

She'd hung sheer curtains and floral drapes at the windows and found a bargain on a secondhand wicker coffee table, which displayed a crystal vase and fresh flowers from Lisa's shop. She'd brought a CD player from home to fill the air with soft, lilting music.

And if her heart broke a little more with every romantic touch she added, not once did Kelsey let that slow her down.

If she had any doubts about her hard work paying off, she'd received encouragement from an unlikely source. When Charlene called earlier, the talk had centered around the rehearsal dinner that night, but nearing the end of the conversation, Charlene had fallen silent before saying, "If I haven't told you before now, Kelsey, I appreciate all you've done for Emily's wedding. We never would have been able to pull this off so quickly if not for you."

After saying goodbye to her aunt, Kelsey hung up the phone and looked around her shop. She had everything she wanted: her shop was up and running, Emily's wedding was only days away and her hard work had gained her aunt's approval.

Congratulations, Kelsey. Your family must be so proud. Seems like you're a real Wilson after all.

Guilt wormed its way through her stomach, but Kelsey pushed it away with a burst of anger as she grabbed her purse and keys. She had no cause to feel guilty, she decided as she locked the front door behind her with a definitive twist of the key. None at all. Connor was the one who'd kept secrets, told lies of omission.

And yet maybe he had a reason. After all, hadn't he encouraged her to consider that her father might have had his reasons for taking the money? At the time, Kelsey thought Connor was talking only about her father. But could Connor have been talking about himself? Hoping that she might understand why he'd taken the ten thousand dollars? And what had she told him?

Nothing he could say would matter, nothing he could do would ever make up for taking the money.

Little wonder, then, that he hadn't bothered with explanations!

She had to talk to Connor, Kelsey decided as she climbed into her car and turned the air on full blast. If she expected him to tell her the truth, she owed it to him to listen without making judgments based on her own past.

Her phone rang, reminding Kelsey that she couldn't drop everything to go see Connor. After the rehearsal, she vowed as she pulled out her cell and flipped it open.

"Kelsey?"

Startled by the unexpected male voice, Kelsey asked, "Yes?"

"It's Javy Delgado. Connor's friend."

"Javy?" She couldn't imagine why he'd call her unless… "Is Connor okay? Has something happened?"

He paused long enough to strip a few years off Kelsey's life before he said, "Do you still care about him?"

"Of course I care about him! I—" *Love him,* Kelsey thought.

"I wasn't sure after the way you treated him."

"The way *I* treated *him?* I know you're Connor's friend, but—"

"Not as good a friend as he's been to me," he interrupted. "And that's why I called even though he asked me not to."

So Connor didn't want to talk to her. He didn't even want his friend talking to her. That didn't give her much hope. "Why wouldn't he want you to talk to me?"

"He doesn't want me to tell you the truth. He's afraid it won't matter. I hope he's wrong about that. About you. Just like you've been wrong about him." Javy sighed. "The money he took, the money your uncle paid him—Connor gave it to my family. He used it to save our restaurant."

* * *

"I have what you need."

Even though Connor had been waiting for the damn call for days, it took him a moment to recognize the voice on the other end. He pushed away from the small table in his hotel room, pent-up energy surging through his veins.

"Jake, it's about time you called. Tell me what you've got is good. I can't wait to get out of this town."

The words were the biggest lie he'd told in the past five minutes. Which was about how long it'd been since he'd last tried to convince himself Kelsey Wilson wasn't worth the effort, and he'd forget all about her the second he got back to California.

"Good? No, I wouldn't call it good," Jake ground out.

Jake sounded nothing like his normal self, and although he and Connor were close, their relationship didn't include a lot of heart-to-heart talks. Still, he had to say, "You sound like hell, man."

"Doesn't matter. I got the job done. I found what I was looking for."

A garbled voice over a loudspeaker sounded in the background. "I have to go. They're calling my flight. I'm e-mailing everything you need right now. Just do me one favor."

"What is it?"

"Use it to nail that guy."

"I will."

"Good. It's about time he gets what he deserves."

As Connor flipped the cell phone closed, his friend's voice rang in his ears. Connor supposed most people would say he was getting what he deserved, too. That Kelsey turning her back on him was just desserts for the way he had taken the money and left Emily years ago.

Except maybe Kelsey's anger wasn't about his relationship

with Emily or the past he couldn't change. Maybe it was about *their* relationship right now, and the truth he'd kept from her.

Okay, yeah, she'd told him nothing could excuse what her father had done when he'd taken money to leave her mother, but maybe if Connor had explained about the Delgados' restaurant...maybe if he'd told her about the money up front so she wouldn't have had to hear about it from *Charlene*, of all people...

Could he really blame Kelsey for reacting the way she had? Between the money her father had taken and the secrets her mother had kept, she had every right to be wary.

Sure, it would have been nice if she'd learned about the money and had still been willing to believe the best about him. But he hadn't placed all his faith in Kelsey, either. He'd been afraid to tell her about the money because he'd feared his reasons—his love and loyalty to the Delgados—wouldn't matter. He'd been holding on to his own past and his own fears that *he* wouldn't matter. He should have trusted her more than that.

His computer e-mail alert sounded, letting him know Jake's report had arrived. A few taps on the keyboard, and Connor understood his friend's anger. "Don't worry, Jake. We've nailed the guy."

After Javy's call, Kelsey longed to turn the car around to go immediately to Connor's hotel, but she couldn't skip the rehearsal, not as Emily's wedding coordinator and not as a member of the Wilson family.

When her phone rang again, her heart skipped a beat as Connor's number flashed across the screen. Still, she hesitated a split second. She wanted to be able to look into his eyes when she apologized. To see that he believed her when she told him she understood why he took the money and she wouldn't expect any less of him than the sacrifice he'd made for his friends.

But after the way she'd treated him, she offered a quick whisper of thanks that he wanted to talk to her at all. Flipping the cell open with one hand, she turned into a nearby parking lot. She immediately sucked in a quick breath, but Connor interrupted any greeting or apology she might have made. "Kelsey, it's Connor. Don't hang up."

She pressed the phone tighter to her ear as if that might somehow bring her closer to Connor. "I'm not. I won't."

"Look, I can explain about the money, I swear—"

"You don't have to—"

"But not now—"

"I talked to Javy—"

"Jake called—"

"What?"

"Jake called. He found Sophia, the Dunworthy's former maid."

Trying to switch gears while her thoughts were going one hundred miles at hour, Kelsey said, "Did he find out why she quit?"

"Turns out she was fired after Dunworthy Senior caught her and Junior together."

"Caught them?"

"From what Sophia says, he'd been hitting on her for months before she finally gave in. Only to lose her job because of it."

"But didn't you say she stopped working for the Dunworthys only a few months ago?" Kelsey asked, mentally going over the timing and coming to an unbelievable conclusion. "Todd and Emily started dating six months ago. They were *engaged* two months ago!"

"Yeah, they were. Evidently sleeping with the maid was the last straw. The way I figure it, Todd proposed to Emily as a way to try to win back his family's approval."

"I can't believe he would do that to Emily!" Anger for her

cousin's sake started to boil inside Kelsey, along with a disgust at the way Todd had smiled and charmed his way into her aunt and uncle's good graces.

"It gets worse."

"Worse! How can it possibly get any worse! Is there someone else?"

"In a way." Connor paused. "Sophia's pregnant."

"Preg—Are you sure the child is Todd's? Considering the money his family has, and after the way Sophia lost her job—"

"Jake is sure of it. He believes her, and I believe him. Judging from his family's reactions, I'd say that the Dunworthys believe it, too. The family doesn't want anything to do with Todd. That's why they aren't here for the wedding." He hesitated. "You were right, Kelsey, and I should have listened to you."

"It doesn't matter now. You did it, Connor. You found the proof you needed."

"Yeah, I've got everything I need," he agreed, his voice sounding hollow. "Look, Kelsey—"

She waited, her heart pounding for everything she wanted to hear, everything she wanted to say. But the silence stretched on, the words unspoken. Finally she said, "The wedding rehearsal is tonight. I'm already on my way to the chapel."

"I'm at the hotel now. I can be there in fifteen minutes."

"Fifteen minutes," Kelsey echoed quietly, before hanging up the phone.

She had fallen in love with the small chapel the first time she saw the cottage-style building, with its cobblestone walls and stained-glass windows. The close proximity to the hotel made it an ideal location. Right now Kelsey wished the chapel were a world away, anything to delay the inevitable end. Once Connor stopped the wedding, he'd have no reason to stick around…and if he did, Kelsey feared it wouldn't be for her.

* * *

Minutes later Kelsey stood inside the empty chapel. It was as beautiful now as when she'd first laid eyes on it. She'd immediately known the perfect arrangement of flowers and candles for alongside the carved pews. Just the right placement of the wedding party on the steps leading to the altar. Exactly where the video and photographer should stand to best capture the light streaming through the windows. She'd known all of that months before Emily had gotten engaged. When Emily had bowed so easily to her suggestions, Kelsey had set in motion the wedding of her own dreams.

She was as guilty as Charlene in pushing her own ideas on Emily. It was *her* dream location for the wedding and reception. All of *her* friends were working side by side to make the day memorable. Maybe if she hadn't been so focused on what she wanted, she would have stopped a long time ago to ask if any of it was what *Emily* wanted.

But she hadn't, and now all their dreams were going down the drain—the perfect wedding to make her business, Emily's dream of marrying the perfect man, Gordon and Charlene's perfect son-in-law. Only Connor had succeeded. He was stopping the wedding as he'd said he would.

He was a man of his word, a good man, and she should have trusted him. Kelsey knew how much it must have hurt when she turned her back on him, just as much as regret and heartache were hurting her now.

A door squeaked behind her, letting in a rush of summer air, and Kelsey took a deep breath. Turning to face her aunt and uncle, she said, "Aunt Charlene, Uncle Gordon, I need to talk to you..." Her voice trailed away when she saw Emily and Todd following a few steps behind.

The one time Kelsey had counted on them being late.

"What is it, Kelsey?" Gordon asked.

"I—" She'd hoped to have a chance to talk to her aunt and uncle alone, to prepare them for what Connor had discovered, so together they could find a way to tell Emily. "I was wondering if I could speak to the two of you in private."

She tried to make the suggestion as casually as possible, but there was nothing casual about the way Charlene's eyebrows arched toward her hairline. "What's wrong? Is it the flowers? The music?"

"Relax, Char," Gordon interjected. "Weren't you saying this morning that Kelsey has everything under control?"

Her uncle's reminder and confident smile sent a sick feeling through Kelsey's stomach. How was she supposed to tell them about Todd?

Taking note of her watching him, Todd crossed his arms over his chest, a not-so-subtle challenge in his expression. "You have something to say, Kelsey?"

She took a deep breath, but before she had chance to speak, the chapel door swung open again. She heard Connor's voice a second before he stepped through the doorway. "Actually, I'm the one with something to say."

"McClane! What are you doing here?" Gordon demanded, a lightning bolt of wrinkles cutting across his thunderous expression.

Todd draped a proprietary arm over Emily's shoulders. "I told Emily inviting him was a mistake. He's still in love with her, and he's probably here because he thinks he can stop the wedding."

"I'm not in love with Emily," Connor insisted.

I'm in love with Kelsey. His heart pounded out the words he never thought he'd say, but damned if he'd say them for the first time with the Wilsons and Todd Dunworthy as witnesses.

He felt the irresistible pull of Kelsey's gaze and he couldn't help meeting her gaze any more than he could resist the earth's gravity. *Not now. Not like this,* he mentally pleaded as he looked into her eyes, willing her to understand.

"Then maybe you'd like to explain *exactly* what is going on here?" Gordon repeated.

This was his moment, Connor thought. His chance to prove he was right and the Wilsons were wrong. Wrong about Todd. Wrong about him. But his triumph rang hollow. He didn't need the Wilsons' approval. He wasn't sure why he'd ever thought he did. All he needed was Kelsey. Her faith. Her trust. Had his past and his secret destroyed that?

"Connor?" Kelsey's voice called to him.

Dressed in a blue-green print dress that hugged her curves, her hair free to curl around her face, she looked absolutely beautiful—strong and vulnerable at the same time, and he couldn't look away.

Whatever Gordon and Charlene saw in his expression had them quickly closing ranks around Kelsey. Surrounded by her aunt and uncle, the Wilson misfit suddenly looked at home within the golden circle, and Connor was alone on the outside.

Tearing his gaze away, he focused on Gordon and pulled the information he'd printed from his back pocket. "Your golden boy has a history of using women. His blue-blood family, who mean so much to you, has completely cut him off after he got one of their maids pregnant." He slapped the pages into Gordon Wilson's reluctantly outstretched hand.

Charlene gasped, color leaching from her face, but doubt pulled Gordon's silver eyebrows together.

"Todd, what is Connor talking about?" Emily asked, her eyes wide as she stared at her fiancé.

"He's lying," Todd scoffed. But instead of trying to console Emily, he looked to Gordon with a can-you-believe-the-nerve-of-this-guy expression. "You know you can't trust anything McClane says."

"But you can trust me, Uncle Gordon," Kelsey insisted as she stepped closer.

"What do you know about this?" her uncle asked, taking a look at the papers.

"I know Connor is a good man." She spoke the words to her uncle, but her gaze never broke from Connor's. "He's here because he's worried about Emily. That information is true."

"Don't listen to her," Todd issued sharply. When Gordon's steely gaze cut his way, filled with the same distrust he'd pinned on Connor's seconds earlier, he quickly backed down. Relaxing his features into a more conciliatory expression, he said, "I'm afraid Kelsey has fallen for McClane's lies, but it's all a smear campaign to stop the wedding."

"How exactly is Connor McClane behind the significant amount of money your family paid this Sophia Pirelli?"

Todd's confident look faded, clay showing through the once-golden facade, but he still didn't give up. "My family let her go, so she went after us for money, claiming the kid she's carrying is mine. The money was a way to keep her quiet."

"A simple paternity test would have done the same thing and been *much* cheaper," Connor pointed out. "The kind of money your family paid… That's not hush money. It's guilt money."

Connor watched with satisfaction as the truth spread across Dunworthy's face and disgust and disappointment over the Wilsons'. Realization hit Emily last, leaving her pale and shaken as she looked from Todd to her parents. Finally her gaze locked with Connor's, and she burst into tears before rushing into his arms.

Seated in Gordon Wilson's study a half hour later, Connor nodded when the older man held up the bottle of scotch. Gordon poured two glasses, handed one to Connor and took a swallow from his own glass before claiming his spot behind the large mahogany desk.

Connor took a sip of his own scotch while he waited for the older man to speak.

"We owe you our thanks," Gordon said after a minute of silence. "When I think of my little girl married to that liar—"

At the chapel Gordon had made it clear to Dunworthy that the engagement was over and the wedding off, and that he'd live to regret it if he ever went near Emily again. Gordon and Charlene had reluctantly agreed to Emily's request that Connor drive her home after Charlene immediately tried to take charge. Emily had surprised them all, demanding some time alone. Connor thought—hoped—that she was learning to stand up for herself.

"I'm glad I found the proof I needed. I only wish I had found it sooner."

"And I wish you had come to me with your suspicions sooner."

Connor couldn't choke back a disbelieving laugh as he set the glass of scotch aside. "I'm not sure how you think that conversation would have played out, but I don't see you taking my side over your handpicked future son-in-law."

"I did not *handpick* Todd. You make it sound like some kind of arranged marriage."

"Wasn't it?"

A flush rising in his face, Gordon struggled for a calming breath. "Look, I'm trying to say that I appreciate what you've done. I don't know how we can repay you."

Pay him…

Shoving to his feet, Connor ground out, "I don't want your money."

"I wasn't offering any," Gordon shot back. He rose to glare at Connor from across the expanse of his desk.

The silent stalemate lasted several tense seconds before Gordon sighed. The tension drained from his body, leaving his shoulders a bit stooped and signs of age lining his face. "Sit back down." He gestured to the leather chair Connor had abandoned. "I've had enough drama for one night."

Hesitating, Connor glanced at the study doorway.

"Expecting someone?"

"I thought Kelsey would be here by now."

In the aftermath of the argument with Dunworthy and Emily's collapse into tears, Connor hadn't had a chance to talk to Kelsey. He'd expected her to head back to the Wilsons' with the rest of her family, where he'd been counting on the chance to talk to her.

But maybe he'd misunderstood what she'd said during the phone call. He should have known Javy wouldn't keep his mouth shut just because he'd told him to, but the more time Connor had to think, the more worried he became. Did her absence mean that Javy's explanation hadn't made a difference? That she still couldn't forgive Connor for the money he'd taken?

Gordon sucked in a deep breath as if preparing for a painful blow and admitted, "I was wrong about Todd."

They were the words Connor had come to Arizona to hear. The perfect lead-in to tell Gordon he hadn't been wrong just about Todd Dunworthy; he'd been wrong about Connor, too. But as he'd already figured out, it no longer mattered. Only Kelsey…

When he stayed silent, the older man repeated, "I was wrong about Todd. I realize now you came back to help Emily, and you have. But you still have some work to do to convince me you're good enough for this family."

"Good enough—" Connor's words broke off when he caught sight of what almost looked like respect gleaming in the older man's blue eyes. Shaking his head and wondering how a single sip of scotch could so seriously impair his judgment, he said, "You don't have to worry about me being good enough. Emily and I are friends. That's all."

As if the night hadn't already been surreal, Gordon Wilson circled his desk to clap a hand on Connor's shoulder. "Who said anything about Emily?" At Connor's surprised glance, Gordon said, "At the chapel I saw the way you were looking at my niece. You never looked at Emily like that. So don't you think it's time for you to go find Kelsey?"

Sitting in her car outside her shop, Kelsey stared at the freshly painted window. Weddings Amour scrolled across the glass in a flowing, curlicued font. The script matched the business cards and letterhead she'd had made—by the thousands, since it was cheaper to buy in bulk.

Kelsey sighed. She should have gone with the rest of her family—and Connor—back to her aunt and uncle's house. But this was Connor's moment. His moment of triumph…of success. And her moment of failure.

Not that Kelsey had expected her cousin to go through with the wedding once she realized Connor was right about Todd. Still, she felt sick with disappointment. She'd worked so hard on the wedding. Her friends had worked so hard! Lisa and Sara… Like her, they had been counting on Emily's wedding, and Kelsey hated letting them down. She dreaded calling them with the news, but that, too, was part of her job. Along with canceling the reservation at the chapel and the hotel reception, phoning all the guests, arranging for gifts to be returned. The mental list went on and on, with Kelsey's hopes and dreams sinking deeper beneath the crushing weight.

But it had to be done, and sitting in her car wouldn't accomplish any of it. Grabbing her purse off the passenger seat, she climbed from the car. As she opened the door to her shop, she tried—and failed miserably—to forget her excitement and gratitude only days earlier as her friends had pitched in to help decorate. The smell of peach potpourri drifted toward her the moment she stepped inside, but it was the memory of Connor's aftershave that filled her senses, playing games with her mind and her heart.

No matter how many unpleasant tasks lay ahead of her, Kelsey would gladly face the professional failure head-on as long as she could turn a blind eye to the personal heartbreak tearing her up inside.

"You should be happy for him," Kelsey whispered as she sank behind her desk and grabbed the box of tissues. She'd placed it there with the idea that a bride might be overcome with emotion and shed some tears of joy. She hadn't anticipated that she'd be sitting alone in her shop, tempted to put her head down and cry.

Connor had done what he'd set out to do. He'd listened to his gut, proved her aunt and uncle wrong, saved the damsel in distress. If life were a Hollywood movie, now would be the time for him to once again ride off into the sunset…this time with Emily.

He said he didn't love her.

But his lack of feeling for Emily wasn't exactly an undying declaration of love for Kelsey. Especially now that Todd was out of the picture and Emily was back in Connor's arms.

She heard the front door swing open and fought back a groan. The sign in the front window still read Closed, but she hadn't remembered to lock the door behind her. She couldn't afford to turn away potential clients, but she'd never felt less like talking about weddings with a head-over-heels-in-love couple.

Pasting on a smile, she pushed away from her desk and walked to the front of the shop. "Can I help…" her voice trailed away as she caught sight of Connor standing in the doorway "*...you?*"

"I hope so." He wore his sunglasses, as he had the first time Kelsey saw him, but the reflective shades didn't offer the protection they once had. She knew now, behind the polished lenses, his eyes were a vivid, vibrant green. Just as she could read the uncertainty behind his cocky smile and the nerves his confident stance—his legs braced wide and arms loose at his sides—couldn't disguise.

Her heart was pounding so hard, Kelsey half expected the shop's glass windows to shake from the force of the vibrations, but only her entire body trembled in reaction. "What are you doing here? I thought you were—"

"With Emily?" he filled in, taking a step farther into the shop.

"She *is* the reason you came back. To stop her from getting married."

"To stop her from getting married to the *wrong* man," he clarified. He took another step forward, and it was all Kelsey could do to hold her ground.

"Are you—" Kelsey licked dry lips and forced the words out, even though they scraped like sandpaper against her throat. "Are you the right man?"

"I like to think so. But not for Emily."

No longer holding her ground, Kelsey was frozen in place as Connor drew closer. His movements slow and deliberate, he stripped off his sunglasses and set them on the wicker coffee table amid the bowl of potpourri and a dozen bridal magazines. Without the glasses, she could see not only his gorgeous green eyes, but the vulnerability and doubt she'd caused with her lack of faith.

"I like to think I'm the right man for you."

Kelsey opened her mouth to agree he was the *only* man for her, but her voice broke on his name and she surprised them both by bursting into tears. Panic crossed Connor's features for a split second before he pulled her into his arms. "It's okay, sweetheart."

Clinging to the warm cotton of his T-shirt and breathing in the sea-breeze scent of his aftershave, Kelsey swallowed against the tears scraping her throat. "I am so sorry, Connor. I should have given you the chance to explain why you took the money. I should have known you would have a good reason, an *honorable* reason."

"I took an easy way out. Don't make it into something it wasn't."

"You were looking out for the Delgados—for your family. I shouldn't have expected anything less."

"And your family was looking out for Emily. I get that now," he said, running a comforting hand up and down her spine. "Besides, I think Gordon and I have an understanding, even if it is going to take a while for your aunt to get used to the idea."

Lifting her head from the comfort of Connor's chest, Kelsey asked, "Wh-what idea?"

"The idea of me and you." His eyes steadily searching her face, he added, "The idea of me loving you."

They were the words Kelsey longed to hear, words she'd thought she would never hear, and she had trouble believing her ears. Surely her imagination had to be playing tricks. Maybe this was nothing but a dream and she'd wake up in her bed—alone—any minute.

"Kelsey?" Connor prompted.

"In my dreams, you're wearing a tuxedo."

Glancing down at his usual jeans and a T-shirt, he swore beneath his breath. "Leave it me to mess this up. Your aunt told me—"

"No, you didn't mess up at all!" Kelsey insisted.

Connor wasn't some fantasy groom who could spout

poetry and had a picture-perfect smile. He wasn't perfect at all. He was real. Loyal and determined, and she loved everything about him—including his bad-boy past. A past that had shaped him into the good man he was now.

"It's perfect and— You talked to my aunt?"

"To your aunt and uncle both. When I asked them for permission to marry you."

Heart pounding crazily in her chest, Kelsey saved wondering about *that* conversation for another time. For now, she could only focus on one thing. "You want to marry me?"

"I love you, Kelsey. I want to spend the rest of my life with you."

"But what about what you said? About love and marriage being nothing but a lie?" she babbled over the voice in her head all but screaming, *Say yes, you idiot!*

"Yeah, well." Looking a little sheepish, he admitted, "I let my parents' relationship color the way I looked at marriage. Of course, my job didn't paint a rosy picture, either. It's one of the things that makes you perfect for me. I'll have you to remind me that sometimes happily-ever-after does come true. That is, if you say yes."

The screaming voice in her head could no longer be silenced, and Kelsey burst out, "Yes, of course. Yes! I love you, Connor. I think I loved you from the minute my aunt showed me your picture and told me it was my job to keep an eye on you. You've been on my mind and in my heart ever since."

The slow smile he gave her was vintage Connor McClane, but the love and tenderness and emotion Kelsey tasted in his kiss…that was brand-new. She clung to his shoulders, never wanting to let him go, and knowing now that she wouldn't have to. He wasn't a man of the moment; he was the man she would love forever.

As Connor slowly eased away, his breath still warming

her lips, his fingers still buried in her hair, he asked, "About your shop... How much damage will Emily canceling the wedding cause?"

It took a second for Kelsey to focus on anything outside the joined circle of their arms. "Well, um, people will understand her calling off the wedding when they find out about Todd. I don't think they'll hold *that* against me. But the chance to show all the guests an amazing wedding and the word-of-mouth publicity the ceremony and reception would have generated, that's a lost opportunity. For me and my friends. I hate disappointing them," she said, a small touch of sadness dimming her joy.

"What if you don't have to?" Connor asked, a familiar gleam in his eyes. The same look he'd had before he suggested they pair up as a team. The kind of look that told Kelsey he was about to offer some crazy solution that just might work.

"What do you mean?"

"I love you, Kelsey. And while I've never thought about it before, I suspect long engagements aren't my style. I want to marry you, and I have it on good authority that the best wedding coordinator in town has the perfect wedding already planned."

"You mean—*Emily's* wedding?" A startled laugh burst from her lips. "You cannot be serious!"

"No?"

"No! I mean, sure, everything's all planned, but it was done for Emily."

"Was it?" he challenged with a knowing lift to his eyebrows. "Was it Emily who insisted on hiring all her friends? Emily who ran around with a hundred lists to make sure every last detail was exactly the way she wanted it?"

How could Kelsey argue when Connor was right? Along the way, the lines had blurred and Kelsey had planned the kind of wedding she'd dreamed about as a starry-eyed, hope-filled little girl, not the kind of wedding she'd dreamed about as a professional career woman.

"Hey, it's just a thought," Connor said. "For all I care, we can go to Vegas or a justice of the peace—"

"Stop!" Kelsey protested in mock horror, even as excitement bubbled inside her like champagne. "A Vegas wedding? If word got out, my career would be over for sure!"

"But what about switching places with the bride? Think your career can withstand that scandal?"

"Well, as long as it's just this once…"

Her words ended in a laugh as Connor spun her around the room. "Oh, I can guarantee we'll only need to do this once," he vowed, love and commitment shining in his eyes.

"You'd really be okay with a big—and I mean, *big*—wedding, with all the Wilson family and friends in attendance?"

Lifting a hand, he traced a pattern on her cheek—the five-point star he'd confessed drove him crazy. But there was only tenderness in his touch as he knowingly said, "They're your friends and family, too."

Kelsey smiled. "You're right. They are." And now that she no longer felt she had to live up to her mother's motto of Wilson women against the world, she knew they would only grow even closer. "And soon they'll be yours, too," she teased with a laugh when Connor groaned. "Are you ready for that and all the happily-ever-after, love-of-a-lifetime, till-death-do-us-part stuff?"

Kelsey could read the answer in Connor's eyes—the promise of a future filled with happily-ever-after.

"With you?" he vowed. "I can't wait."

* * * * *

RICK'S APPOINTMENT with his attorney early Wednesday morning went only moderately better than his meeting with social services the day before. The prognosis wasn't great—but at least his attorney was going to file a motion for DNA testing. Just so Rick could petition to see the child...his sister's baby. The sister he didn't know he had until it was too late.

The rest of what his attorney said had been downhill from there.

Cell phone in hand before he'd even reached his Nitro, Rick punched in the speed dial number he'd programmed the day before.

Maybe foster parent Sue Bookman hadn't received his message. Or had lost his number. Maybe she didn't want to talk to him. At this point he didn't much care what she wanted.

"Hello?" She answered before the first ring was complete. And sounded breathless.

Young and breathless.

"Ms. Bookman?"

"Yes. This is Rick Kraynick, right?"

"Yes, ma'am."

"I recognized your number on caller ID," she said, her voice uneven, as though she was still engaged in whatever physical activity had her so breathless to begin with. "I'm sorry I didn't get back to you. I've been a little…distracted."

The words came in more disjointed spurts. Was she jogging?

"No problem," he said, when, in fact, he'd spent the better part of the night before watching his phone. And fretting. "Did I get you at a bad time?"

"No worse than usual," she said, adding, "Better than some. So, how can I help?"

God, if only this could be so easy. He'd ask. She'd help. And life could go well. At least for one little person in his family.

It would be a first.

"Mr. Kraynick?"

"Yes. Sorry. I was…are you sure there isn't a better time to call?"

"I'm bouncing a baby, Mr. Kraynick. It's what I do."

"Is it Carrie?" he asked quickly, his pulse racing.

"How do you know Carrie?" She sounded defensive, which wouldn't do him any good.

"I'm her uncle," he explained, "her mother's—Christy's—older brother, and I know you have her."

"I can neither confirm nor deny your allegations, Mr. Kraynick. Please call social services." She rattled off the number.

"Wait!" he said, unable to hide his urgency. "Please," he said more calmly. "Just hear me out."

"How did you find me?"

"A friend of Christy's."

"I'm sorry I can't help you, Mr. Kraynick," she said softly. "This conversation is over."

"I grew up in foster care," he said, as though that gave him some special privilege. Some insider's edge.

"Then you know you shouldn't be calling me at all."

"Yes… But Carrie is my niece," he said. "I need to see her. To know that she's okay."

"You'll have to go through social services to arrange that."

"I'm sure you know it's not as easy as it sounds. I'm a single man with no real ties and I've no intention of petitioning for custody. They aren't real eager to give me the time of day. I never even knew Carrie's mother. For all intents and purposes, our mother didn't raise either one of us. All I have going for me is half a set of genes. My lawyer's on it, but it could be weeks—months—before this is sorted out. Carrie could be adopted by then. Which would be fine, great for her, but then I'd have lost my chance. I don't want to take her. I won't hurt her. I just have to see her."

"I'm sorry, Mr. Kraynick, but…"

* * * * *

Find out if Rick Kraynick will ever have
a chance to meet his niece.
Look for A DAUGHTER'S TRUST
by Tara Taylor Quinn,
available in September 2009.